All Screwed Up

Michael Nsonwu

Published by New Generation Publishing in 2012

First Edition

www.newgeneration-publishing.com

New Generation Publishing

Prologue

The first three chapters deal with the author's history and the attack on him by his colleagues.

The remaining five chapters represent the fallout after the killing of an innocent African inmate by overzealous and prejudiced prison officers, and show the radical, emotional and spiritual changes the experience brought on the author.

Identifying more with the rehabilitative format in Pentonville prison, he becomes something of a hero in his compassionate understanding of their cause and his unorthodox approach towards their rehabilitation. This causes considerable envy among his peers, as he is one of the few prison officers that inmates go to great lengths to seek out for moral and professional support.

At the end of the day, concerned with the leadership power Michael wields over the inmates, who are keen to subject themselves to his approach to justice and rehabilitation, his fellow officers close ranks against him, intending to remove him from the system. This appears to be the motive of the brutal beating to which he was subjected in the first chapter.

The book gives a step by step chronological guide to the further frustrations Michael encounters in his every effort to seek redress, all the way up to the High Court where, although his case was filed, to this day he has not been accorded a hearing.

This appalling indictment against one of the most civilised penal systems in the world is set against the background of a European society which prides itself as being one of the most tolerant in the world.

~

Acknowledgements

This book took 13 years to get to this point, during this time I have been blessed with a wife, Jennifer and three wonderful children, Nina, Kiki and Michael III.

Meanwhile we have seen society deteriorate and sadly some of the predictions in the book have come true.

I would like to acknowledge the following:

Dilibe Onyeama for his wonderful help.
Munir Zaman for his belief and help in making this real.
Toby Osbourne for his fine editorial skills.
My late father Michael Oguzie Nsonwu, Ichie Onyeukwu Oka Ome I of Amucha, for being my father in every sense of the word.

And finally to the source of all creation, my father who art in heaven, who in every culture and race is named differently but yet is the same.

All Screwed Up

by Michael Nsonwu

Everybody has a story to tell. A man's story is his very life. Now I, personally, have this golden opportunity to present my life, my case before the court of World Public Opinion - to the end that the power of injustice may be curbed.

Yes, this is my story. Though, I am more than aware of Groucho Marx's claim: "When a person starts writing his memoirs, it's a sure sign he's washed up!"

To this, I laugh. "Screwed up" I may be, but not washed up.

~

Chapter One

'Laws are like cobwebs, which may catch small flies but let wasps and hornets break through'

~ Jonathan Swift

Manufacturing monsters. The prison system is a vicious circle, a downward spiral of infinite design; crime and violence breed together behind the bars, growing like a virus on a Petri dish.

As a prison officer for Her Majesty's prisons for six years, I've done my time. Inmates call you a 'Screw' and threaten physical harm. Yet, I never expected that the worst beating in my entire life would be at the hands of my fellow employees, the other officers I worked with.

I lay there, confused at the sudden turn of events, in a pool of my own blood, defenceless to their ongoing assault. Four on one; at least four. Fists raining down on my body. What had I done to deserve this? Was it because of my heritage (born to a Scottish mother and Nigerian father)? Was it because of my race? Or was it because I could see right through them?

My whole demeanour had changed ever since the day that Lumumber died. Two years prior to my cruel beating, I saw him being taken away by prison officers – that was the last time I saw him alive. 'Unlawful killing' was the verdict. That's when I started to see things differently. Really differently.

I have always held an outlook that is perhaps more philosophical than the other officers in the prison service. I raised eyebrows and asked questions. Sometimes sticky questions, which perhaps would result in my eventual exit from my employment – effectively disabled out of injury and reaction to the farce that surrounded the eventual fates of my attackers…

Without warning, in the early hours of December 17th 1994, the pain would be instantaneous and unbearable. Moments before this life-changing turn of events, I was bored but intact. It was a cool night, and upon collecting my blue overcoat from the bar, I scanned the crowd of some 150 good-time colleagues and guests who were partying, with Christmas joy, at the annual bash hosted by the administrative department of Her Majesty's Prison, Pentonville.

The music was loud, and my vision squinty, against the cigarette smoke and depth of the hall. Where the hell was Ike? He had promised me a lift and I was relieved to be going home soon. These official functions always left me cold, but I'd been touched that the entry fee would be donated to charity and had promised the admin staff my attendance in acknowledgement of our good working relationship.

An officer I knew vaguely as David approached me with a toothy smile. "Hi Mick, can I have a word?" He put his arm around my shoulder, steering me towards the exit.

The season of goodwill. "Sure," I replied, thinking nothing of it. We stepped out into the half-lit corridor between the function hall and the bar, the atmosphere contrasting with the animated mood of gaiety and bonhomie emanating from the festivities.

As I turned my face, David grabbed me by the throat. His nails scrapped mywind pipe and his grip began to close. Then, both of my arms were locked in a classic 'control and restraint' manoeuvre (one of the techniques developed bythe Prison Service to control violent inmates - usually involving three officers, two controlling the arms in wrist locks and the third cradling the head to avoid injury in the course of the struggle)From behind.

I gasped, partlyin shock but mostlydue to the abrupt restriction on my air. It was all so sudden, so unexpected. Initially, I was more taken aback than frightened. Of course, it must be a practical joke. A stupid and thoughtless practical joke; the result of too much booze and heightened sense of camaraderie. Right?

Looking bleakly around within the limits of my constriction for a smiling face or even straining my ears for a jolly laugh, it was only when I clapped my eyes on David's malice-filled pupils that I realised his whole face was an unmistakable mask of menace. I was paralysed on the spot even before I was pinned on both sides by the locks, held rigidly upright by my throat. In my confusion and panic, I started to struggle; a natural instinct when trapped and unable to budge.

As the hopelessness of my situation washed over me, a voice in my head squeaked, "Why?" - knowing that it was a question that was unlikely to ever be answered.

~

The slam of the metal doors. The stale smell of the cells. The prisoners who bite and shout.

I've seen the new inmates arrive; sentenced for petty non-violent crimes, later emerging from prison as hardcore criminals; more violent than before, a product of the system.

Should I be surprised that the officers, like sponges, are soaked in this violence, too? After a while, you either accept it, or object to it. I would opt for the latter, ultimately, much to the dismay of my superiors; no wonder they wanted me gone. But, really, had it come to this?

With one hand, being offered drinks and a meal to say 'Merry Christmas' and with the other hand, plunging a knife into my still-beating heart...

~

As I struggled, I should have recognised the futility of such action, room for any effective movement was too small, the pressure on my throat defied resistance, and the locks on my arms were utterly disabling.

With rank breath that reeked of whiskey and hatred, my assailants were tough and brawny, as befits those eligible for law enforcement in the penal system, which hardly entertains dainty Cinderellas.

Recognising my horrifying predicament, I heard myself cry out my internal concerns: "What? Why?" With the grip on my throat allowing minimal movement I was forced to look into David's hate filled eyes. He began to breathe heavily and next thing David's forehead smashed into my face just above the left cheekbone. My head felt as if it would split in half. The pain came in waves as he continued to butt me in the face like an enraged rhino. On the fourth assault, time went into slow motion as an inner voice screamed a chilling realisation – "These guys mean to kill you!"

Call it some primordial survival instinct, call it training or intuition, I went limp and as the grips on my arms slackened, using the wall behind me as a springboard, I lunged forward suddenly and grabbed

David by his throat, in a final desperate attempt.

David gave a surprised yelp, screaming, "Get him off me!" He was falling backwards. Falling. Falling.

We hit the ground in a tangled heap. As more blows pummelled me, I tucked myself into a ball, another instinct, as well as a planned manoeuvre to present a smaller target.

Then, in the ensuing pandemonium, one of the side doors burst open and presented a miraculous escape route. The light poured over me and I moved towards it. I dived out.

~

Many times, I've been threatened with

bodily harm. In the course of my work as a prison officer, it's a risky business.

I had initially been inspired to make a constructive contribution towards easing the plight of the kind of people I knew and grew up with, and consequently was encouraged to enter the prison service in 1990, little believing that I myself would ultimately become the victim of the kind of vicious delinquency I had come to purge inmates of - by fellow officers of all people! And to cap it all, their criminality would be denied all the way up the halls of justice.

Here it was, death staring me so closely in the face. After all the 'bad men' I've seen incarcerated, I had never even given a second thought of an attack outside of the prison, an unprovoked attack by the 'good men' who supposedly protect our society from the worst criminals.

Dostoyevsky, the author of Crime and Punishment, once observed that: “The degree of civilisation in a society can be judged by entering its prisons.”

In Britain, we have approximately 77,000 inmates in captivity; in fact, we imprison more people per head of population than any other European country. And what would Dostoyevsky assess as the “degree of civilisation” that is apparent from these jails?

Well, on that fateful night of my attack, I can only imagine that he would think us a pack of animals. Especially when you consider that we were the officers of the prisons, and not the criminals, at each others’ throats.

I just wanted to know 'why?' I was being mob-attacked. Why did they want me dead? Although, in my heart, I knew the writing was on the wall – after Lumumber, my change, my outspokenness. Like a fly in their soup, I had to go.

~

Rubbing his neck, my fingers leaving red imprints on his skin, David picked himself up, clearly unnerved by my effective counterattack. Looking down, he grabbed a bottle.

Following behind me, he smashed it and came at me, hands raised in readiness to strike, but was wrestled to the ground by several party guest onlookers who had by now arrived at the scene.

Adrenaline was still pumping wildly as I stood there shouting, "Why? Why! What did I do wrong?"

My left cheekbone was streaming blood; open from the impact of David's head butts. The vision in my left eye felt impaired, and it seemed as if the eye itself was half-closed, adding to my unsteadiness.

Through the chaos and din, I heard my friend Ike and several other officers anxiously asking me: "What on earth is happening?"

"Tell us, Michael, what's been going on here?"

"Was someone drunk? There's obviously been a fight."

Bewildered, I tried to describe the mob-attack and as I did so I saw one of my attackers, Peter, walking out of another door, out of the staff club. "There's one of them," I shouted, moving to grab him.

Peter started hurling punches like a demented demon. People tried to separate us. Everybody seemed to end up on the floor. Peter grabbed my jaw, inserted his fingers in my mouth and tried to yank my lower jaw apart. I bit down to ease the pressure. All hell broke loose. Officers were screaming at each other. Ike was shouting obscenities at them.

Seemingly moments later, but it could have been longer, the police arrived, about half a dozen officers. "What's going on?"

Half of my face caked in blood, I looked at the officer with my one good eye. "David and his mates cornered me, out of the blue, no reason, beat me up."

"Go and check the staff club, see if they are in there," ordered the senior police officer.

A few minutes later David was brought out, handcuffed, and led away. He looked back at me, calmly.

"We need to escort you to the station for a medical examination, you look a right mess. And you'll need to make a statement."

I nodded; a swollen, achy nod. The hall started moving away from me, or I was moving away from it. The night air, the cold night air, hit my skin, almost stinging the blood and cuts.

The road whizzed past the windows of the police car as I rode in the back seat. Street lights blurred around me.

At the station, stares and nods as I walked in and was ushered away from sight. I was treated and examined by the duty doctor, then shown to an office and told to wait.

I heard that David was formally charged with Actual Bodily Harm. He was 'processed' (his belongings taken off him) and then locked in a cell.

Some twenty minutes of waiting later, a police constable came into the office and sat opposite me, with a notepad, ostensibly to write down my evidence. But as I started recounting my ordeal, I noticed he was not taking down any notes. Even though the very act of talking was taking every ounce of energy from my sore body and mind, he just sat there, poker-faced, as he started picking at my story. In the face of my insistence, he accused me of being stubborn. We started to argue, and he left.

A few minutes later a sergeant came in. First he offered cigarettes, which I declined; then he offered coffee, which I didn't want either. His manner was rather patronising when he said, "Michael - may I call you Michael?"

"Sure."

"You seem to be a man of the world." He smiled, but his eyes were cold. "Do you catch my drift?"

"I'm not sure I do."

"Oh come on, you don't want your fellow officers to go to jail and lose their jobs, do you? Come on now, we are all officers - *esprit de corps* and all that, you know." He gave me a cheeky wink.

"I understand what you are saying," I told him. "But, I want to find out why I was attacked. The manner of attack was so brutal and I'm entitled to know what I did to deserve being treated as an animal."

The sergeant pursued the same line of forgive and forget, even though he was at a loss to justify the attack. Finally, he told me to relax while he briefly took care of a few things.

This was my first opportunity to reflect after this whirlwind of pain and turbulence. One moment at a party, the next moment thrown headfirst into a nightmare. Had I been guilty of any terrible wrongdoing? I wracked my brain and tried to remember if there was anything I had said and done which would merit what had happened to me.

As a Christian, both in orientation and in practice, I am a keen advocate of letting bygones be bygones - within reason. Equally, I am aware that revenge is a human instinct and that in the whirlwind of violent emotions - such as I felt during my encounter with David and his mates - there is the tendency to pluck out an eye for every eye plucked out.

Yet, after the storm subsides and rational thought takes over, it would be expected of men of reason to draw a distinction between emotional revenge and cool reprisal. If the event is unjustified, then there is nothing wrong with revenge if seen in the light of a warning to the offender not to repeat the offence. In such a situation, the principle of an eye for an eye becomes perfectly in order, if only as a deterrent to protect society.

Only in the principle of a tooth for a tooth for the mere sake of healing injured pride does revenge not become a reprisal, but a crime against God. Right, now if I could not establish a justifiable reason for my ordeal, I was bent on David and his accomplices facing the full wrath of the law. Thus, I sat in quiet contemplation.

Five minutes after the sergeant had left, the constable who had first interrogated me reappeared, accompanied by Peter. The constable showed me a little mark on Peter's finger, cleared his throat and declared that if I were not willing to drop the charges, the police would be forced to arraign me as well on an assault charge.

I could not believe what I just heard. "But, he was one of the people who attacked me!" I protested with unsteady belligerence.

"Makes no difference," answered the constable in a callous manner that somehow amplified his slight Cockney accent, and made a mockery of the air of authority and rectitude conveyed by his uniform. I looked beyond the uniform, considered the mean expression of his somewhat pinched, rugged features and a face that had suddenly been unmasked, showing a total disregard for the truth. I saw a 'bent copper' and this was infinitely more distressing than an ordinary civilian rogue.

"We will have to lock you up!" the constable declared. "To be honest, I don't think we can guarantee your safety."

Chilled and outraged by his words, I had to summon a vast amount of patience not to strangle him. The reality of the situation hit me like a ton of bricks. Here I was, at about three o'clock on a Sunday morning at Islington Police Station, talking with the police, to whom I had come for justice and protection, who were now telling me that unless I withdrew the charges, they were going to institute counter-charges and that anything could happen to me.

My mind was in a spin; I was at a loss as to what to do. But most important of all, I was intimidated. The trap of blackmail had effectively been sprung.

"You haven't heard the last of this," I vowed under my breath with contempt. "Okay, you win, I'll withdraw the charges."

They were getting away with it.

This is the 'law and order' that I represent? This is my team? *Esprit de corps?* More like the 'Blue' wall. Protecting themselves instead of the victim – in this case, me.

~

I was hell-bent on taking my case to the Prison Authorities, investing in faith that truth and justice would ultimately prevail. With that naïve fundamental logic, I withdrew the assault charges and went home to lick my wounds. Yet, some of my injuries were far from external.

My friend Ike, who had been waiting in the duty hall, drove me to my home at Palmers Green, in North London. He shared my rage and suggested that he should take photographs of my injuries; he had brought a camera to the party. Ike kept me company for the rest of the night.

After he left, I telephoned the Senior Officer of my Wing at Pentonville, since I was supposed to be on duty that morning. He had already been apprised of the incident, and voiced his support of my reporting the attack to the Prison Authorities.

But the police law enforcer was not concerned that a crime had been committed as such, but that it had been perpetrated by another agent of law enforcement. Therefore, the 'system' which employed them both was on trial, and the embarrassment resulting from the mere prosecution - let alone a court conviction - would have proved disastrous to the administration. I could smell a cover-up on the horizon...

~

In my naivety, expecting ultimate redress from higher agents of the same system, I could not have envisaged that the conspiracy of silence which masqueraded first in the crocodile smile of the fatherly sergeant who wanted to call me Michael, and then the more aggressive, more intimidating approach of his emissary the constable, would represent the pattern of my encounters all the way up the establishment ladder.

Excerpts from notes taken at the disciplinary hearing held at HMP Pentonville give credence to this line of thought -

Chairman: There is another problem which you are aware of Mr Turner, I'm sure some of the policemen involved on the night have been very vocal about their opinions about what the hell was going on or not going on, not just at this prison but across London and therefore I think it is inadmissible to take any statements from the police in this regard. I know about it, I have heard about it from senior policemen, I do not want to hear about it formally.

Mr Turner (the Prison Officers Association representative): What, this incident?

Chairman: Yes. The police have no role to play, if they had a role it was in terms of charging people.

Mr Turner: Then the decision was made by the officers not to pursue it.

Chairman: Still, the police did have a choice, mark you, but there is some feeling about that amongst the local Bobbies as well.

Mr Turner: I think we are all in each other's hands here. I have got to be quite honest, in 25 years I have never seen such a mess.

Chairman: Yes, a bit of a shambles springs to mind.

~

For me, it all became a do-or-die battle to install truth in the corridors of power; little knowing that it was destined to be the most daunting challenge of my life. It became like searching for water in the desert, the entire process beautified with niceties of diplomatic charm which the British have moulded into a fine art. The refinement of civilised dialogue - accompanied by that mesmerising deceptive smile, as can be found on a shark before it inflicts that fatal bite, and the captivating wonder of superior diction embellishing a careful presentation of logic - is certain to disarm any aggrieved complainant.

As H L Mencken so acutely observed, "The penalty for laughing in a Courtroom is six months in jail; if it were not for this penalty, the jury would never hear the evidence."

If it is the spirit and not the form of law that keeps justice alive, as Earl Warren sees it, then the learned 'Earl' might bear in mind that such logic might not apply to the British people...

Having now registered that indictment against the British system, what was the truth I was bent on establishing? From the moment of the attack, I had been desperately trying to establish a motive held by David and his cohorts. After all, it could all have been some terrible mistake, like mistaken identity.

At the police station I had embarked on a process of elimination. Had I enjoyed an affair with a fellow officer's wife or mistress? No. Had I betrayed some vital secret? No. Had I duped someone? No. Yet these misdemeanours seemed the most likely causes for a mob attack of such brutal savagery.

In the course of pursuing the matter with higher authorities, though, I was amazed to learn that David had woven some fantastic yarn to the police that I had been making advances toward his girlfriend (who was a prison service nurse). This complete fabrication, which was ultimately dismissed by the police, went through several stages of amendment in the ensuing internal investigations before dying a quiet death. Among the host of witnesses who testified, no girlfriend appeared to verify such a story. Nobody else saw me pursuing a woman - successfully or otherwise - and even if some fine thread of truth could be attached to this concoction, it would not have been under coercion, in the sense that successful 'chatting up' can hardly be a one-sided show. Even had it been so, surely a stiff warning and possibly a wallop to the jaw should have sufficed?

Could a mere 'chatting up' session have been sufficient cause for a supposedly responsible prison officer, in the essence of his calling, schooled in self-discipline and self-control, to engage in the criminal conspiracy of procuring the assault and actual bodily harm of a fellow officer? Was a 'chatting up' session of such monumental grievance as to warrant near lynching?

What times these are. Sad and desperate times. As a result, it is on record that when David was interviewed by Governor Mason on the 16th February 1995 and was asked, "Did you at any time during this incident, have a glass or a bottle in your hand?" he answered, "I have been advised by my Association not to answer any further questions. I have nothing to add."

The long and short of everything was that inasmuch as Governor Mason observed that the claim of 'chatting up' could be regarded as a prima facie "motive" for attack, the credibility of the claim simply broke down under cross-examination. I was in no doubt that it was a hastily invented defence to draw attention away from the real motive behind the incident. The fact that Mr Turner first represented me and then represented my attackers (in other words took evidence from me and then went to my attackers and concocted a defence) only served to strengthen my final conviction that it was more in line with a conspiracy. Moreover, this was a conspiracy of which higher authorities inside Pentonville were in the know, and the cover-up by the police did nothing to allay my fears…

In the years to come, I would ponder the facts and wonder: what <u>was</u> the real motive? I would also see myself face the jaded reality of prison life, where prisoners would enter the system, to be contaminated further by the effluence of addictions and habits and new 'bad influences,' leaving worse than before; worsening themselves in society, effectively.

Above all else, I drew inevitable conclusions about my own case, as I learned to see the world again, through these new eyes, this new vision. I was satisfied that it was not unrelated to the British attitude to colour.

A Brit above all, with natural aesthetic disposition, appreciates the golden colour of a glorious sunset emblazoned across the sky - and indeed its radiant splendour would not go unnoticed anywhere in the world - but those of the 'Paki-bashers, Nigger-hunters and Wogs begin at Calais' persuasion do not feel such sweet intoxication when that miraculous hue is reflected on the skin of a human being, as it is with me. **I am not Black, I am not White either, I am a Human Being.**

The Brits who are afflicted with pretence of bigotry, when assessing any non-thoroughbred British native, might make allowances for any <u>European</u> whose nationality was not obvious at first sight, but come down hard on citizens of varying hue from other continents. In this regard, the native Brit is at his weakest, still smarting from the death of his imperial glory and mentally re-living it with such wistfulness as to act it out through policies that should have been phased out with the Empire.

As the subjects of that former Empire are at the receiving end of these policies, the native Briton may indict himself subconsciously, but will go to any extreme to shield this festering weakness from public view. He has made it exceedingly difficult for any change to be sustained with any hope of success.

Certainly, with that imperious air, the universally-acclaimed English language and diction, the subtle, meticulous manner and the aptitude for logic and deduction, the Brit has a formidable asset that can blind the finest legal luminary bent on exposing that weakness.

Every institution created ostensibly to placate aggrieved members of racial minorities are, in effect, masterful defence tactics to protect and preserve colonial attitudes, one could argue. And I had to find this out the hard way through direct personal encounters, having been a long-time casual observer.

My fight for redress against my assailants amounted to a fight against the British system, with subtle obstacles being erected at every turn. As one of my aids from the Commission For Racial Equality told me while we were preparing the

Industrial Tribunal case, "We work on percentages - only 10% of those who apply are prioritised and represented and out of that only 10% of those represented actually win and this is CRE policy." He went on to describe it as "lifting the lid off the pressure cooker to let off steam."

~

A tape recording of my cross-examination of Governor Mason, containing vital evidence in my favour, developed feet when it was urgently required and strayed out of sight, never to be seen again. I was told however that a written copy of the tape was found on a typist's machine.
I had always assumed that such cover-up tactics characterised the crude survival strategies of Third World governments, but it was clear that wherever a worm turns, it

is still a worm.

I was forced to witness at first hand that it was permissible to indict the British with every kind of shortcoming - from being a snob to a disposition for kinky sex - but **never ever** call him a racist... It's just not cricket.

'Racism' became the final theme of my war for redress, and the calibre of opponents in the course of the battle somehow evokes vivid impressions of the plight of the oppressed but valiant black tenant in confrontation with his villainous white landlord in Langston Hughes' poetic classic *Ballad of the Landlord.* A portion of the poem reads:

Police! Police!
Come and get this man!

All Screwed Up ~ Michael Nsonwu

He's trying to ruin the Government
And overturn the land

Copper's whistle!
Patrol Bell!
Arrest.
Precinct Station
Iron cell.
Headlines in Press:
Man threatens landlord
Tenant held no bail
Judge gives Negro 90 days
In county jail

At the end of that bitter two-year struggle, culminating in my abrupt and premature retirement from Her Majesty's Service for no rational reason - I actually found myself 'medically retired' without going through any kind of medical examination - I became all screwed up!

I headed for the Courts, only to learn that pure and simple truth about British justice; it's not blind, but it is rarely simple or black and white. I had inadvertently become an example of French author Francois de la Rochefoucauld's words: "The love of justice in most men is only the fear of themselves suffering injustices." In my quest for practical fulfilment of that love, I ended up sharing Lenny Bruce's discovery: "In the halls of justice, the only justice is in the halls."

I was left with no other option than to head for the court of public opinion, inspired in no small measure by the prison misadventures of Henri Charriere in *Papillon*. But while he was an inmate, and I was an officer; one of us held involuntarily, the other a voluntary worker; in neither case was it the principle of hardship and endurance behind bars in which lends moral or message to the story. It was not the relationship with prisoners, with officers and prison governors. In Charriere's case, it was the horrendous barbarity of a French penal system, which was unbecoming of a country of the status of France. No less so with the British.

Charriere would try to fly away like a butterfly, while I was deemed an ongoing threat, buzzing in their faces, that needed to be swatted…

~

The dramatic incident which shattered my career when white officers closed ranks against me, the murderous sense of injustice it fired inside me, and my dogged but vain efforts to exact befitting retribution through the legal process, are merely incidental.

The solid base from where I am making a sweeping review of a penal system which, far from the purifying effects expected from its tentacles on the hardened criminal, has displayed a startling disregard for the sanctity of human life. If we do not hold those who are officers in the prison, and police service, to a higher standard than the 'scum' in the cells, then what have we become? Who are we?

Tragically, very few reformed characters emerge from the gates of Pentonville after amassing their relevant period of incarceration; physically they may appear the same, but mentally they are monsters in the making.

There has been a growing trend in youth culture to look at a prison experience as an acceptable part of being 'hip' or 'hard.' Peer pressure and drug culture has made the present-day youth especially vulnerable to this type of negative influence.

The efforts of Prison Authorities to improve conditions, rather than pursue a rehabilitative format, created a dependent attitude on the part of the inmates. Inevitably the general attitude has been this typical carefree retort: "I could do time standing on my head."

Doing time is now regarded as a fashionable accessory of street credibility. In the light of the immense impact of incarceration on the individual, there is the need to correct this impression. The chilling reality sees individuals going to prisons most often for innocuous charges - only to come out with the habits of hardened criminals. It's not a walk in the park in there. You will be reformed, but unlikely it will be any kind of transformation other than degradation and devolution to a primal state.

One need not stretch one's imagination to appreciate the disastrous implications of this development for our youth. A survey of the family life of ex-convicts will substantiate this. Misleading is the consensus of opinion stating that 'He has changed since he went to prison.' Changed in what way? For the better? A truly reformed character? This change cannot be overstated; it leads to an avenue of lower esteem, lower expectations, a creation of a 'them and us' divide which invariably branches off to the dark recesses of a criminal fraternity, a sub-culture.

A glaring reality for the non-white inmates of Pentonville prison was the inability of the white officers to dissemble their supremacist attitudes, sometimes with tragic consequences. Lumumber, poor Lumumber... For the non-white inmates in Britain, prison is an intensification of the purgatory of trying to survive in British society.

This then is the essence of my story; my life: we are students every second of our lives, there is no end to learning, and there is no end to improvement. This philosophy is set against the insider background of one man's experience behind bars in what is supposedly the most civilised penal system in the world. It is a story of a decadent former colonial power whose inability to reconcile to the loss of her colonies largely gave rise to the growing decadence, and in that decadence the former subjects of the Third World colonies can never be regarded as equal citizens except before God - and it is conceivable that the British might never accept even that qualification. Surely, they will continue to devise better and more effective approaches to dissembling their attitudes, but those attitudes will not change.

Thus, even now, I feel like I am standing on the outside of the bars, looking in...
This is my story.

Chapter Two

"In this bright future, you can't forget your past."

~ Bob Marley

Like most good stories, one must start at the beginning – 1959.

It was an important year. In January, the Cuban capitalist dictator Batista resigned and fled to Miami, paving the way for Fidel Castro, the rebel leader, to move in and capture Santiago. Upon taking over, Castro emphasised that his revolution in Cuba was humanistic rather than communist

In April, Mao Tse Tung resigned as China's Head of State in favour of Liu Shao-chi, but remained chairman of the

Chinese Communist Party.

In June, Singapore became independent, with Lee Kuan Yew as Prime Minister of the republic.

On July 5th, President Sukarno dissolved the constituent assembly of Indonesia, moving steadily to a more authoritarian regime.

And a couple days later, on July 7th, Michael Oguzie Nsonwu was born in the bleak industrial town of Blantyre, just outside Glasgow, Scotland.

In contrast to Nigeria's 140 million people; Blantyre boasts a population of 17,000, the streets rife with gangs and dereliction. Blantyre is best known as the birthplace of David Livingstone ("Dr Livingstone, I presume?") the famous explorer and missionary. But, not so well known as the birthplace of me.

In fact, of all the many historic names above, *who the hell is Michael Oguzie Nsonwu?*

Well, apart from Dr Livingstone, law enforcement is their common thread. One way or another each represented rebellion against a system that had seen the triumph of injustice over fair play, and each sought to enforce change in the most expedient manner possible.

Years later, I was to clash with a system in which injustice reared its ugly features. A many-armed beast when battling against its inner-workings and those who oil the cogs and gears. Leaving the individual to be caught in the merciless machinery.

Nevertheless, it was only much later that it dawned on me; the cryptic motive behind the resistance to my perseverance to install truth was that very 'rebel' instinct of my constitution - a diehard tenacity that supported my eligibility for the duty of law enforcement in the first place.

While it was gratifying to be recognised by the establishment, it was understandably no source of joy to have to turn that 'asset' against the very establishment that claimed to be a symbol of justice. I wanted to slap on the bracelets and haul away this unjust enterprise, now that I found myself facing the dirty end of the proverbial stick.

Was my employment by that system some unspoken agreement that if the system itself breached its own rules, the law enforcer should look the other way? Even if that means disregarding injustice that inflicts injury on myself, another law enforcer?

As the law which I sought to enforce on the system involved an area in which the system was loathed to confront itself, it was looking as though I would suffer. I was evidently in a no-win situation, but nothing short of death was going to stand in my way. Maybe if the whole world could be kin - that is to defy even death in order that truth may prevail - there would be global peace. That is grandioso wishful thinking, however, and I was never disposed to unrealistic expectations, I merely recognised that difficult things take a long time, the impossible a little longer.

Certainly, I was not the first 'non-native' to try to take on the system, and doubtless I would not be the last. But, where the 'powers that be' became unstuck in my case was the wrongful assumption that my circumstances mirrored those of the vast majority of lowly citizens of colour who could easily be dispensed with if they refused to toe the line, by the very fact of their dependence on the goodwill of the establishment for their survival.

In such instances, such temporary rebellions amounted to little more than storms in teacups, permanently silenced, with the victims relegated to the wretchedness of dole life and permanent obscurity. In the absence of a cushy background to prop them up in the event of defeat, their fall from grace would come early in the struggle, surely?

If otherwise the victim maintains the strength and guts to soldier on, and ends up remaining in the system after some sort of compromise, such compromise would fall into the pigeonhole of what is popularly known as 'buying off.' Not so in this case, unknown to the powers-that-be.

There was no price on my head, no compromise available.

~

When my father met my mother in Scotland in 1958, he was a 29-year-old student of mechanical engineering and my mother an 18-year-old grocer's assistant from a poor working class background. My mother was Scottish, of the same complexion, radiance and openness as the moon. When the light of the moon was obscured by the blanket of clouds, my father's ebony Nigerian hue merged unseen with the darkness of the night. The privacy provided allowed the couple to damn the myopic attitudes of the segregationists and forge a healthy oneness, from which they were accorded a golden compromise - me.

Ultimately, my mother was ostracised by absolutely everyone for having committed the double sin of bearing a child out of wedlock, and for having so 'let the side down' as to kiss and love across the colour line.

I have no memories of my mother because my father, on completing his studies in 1961, tricked her into releasing me and spirited me away to Nigeria. I was just two years old. I am sure he was mainly motivated by compassion, wanting to spare us both from further social stigma. (This would not have been a problem in Nigeria, where colour variations among my father's Ibo stock were common, from light olive to the deepest black, with albinos being common.)

My mother, I was later told, made strenuous efforts to hunt us down in Nigeria with the aim of taking me back to Scotland, but was frustrated by the Nigerian system, which my father used to his advantage. Foreigners would find the bureaucratic red-tape unfathomable and, unlike Scotland, my father would be favoured with a home-court advantage.

Thus, in later years, I would look back on the cards the hands of fate had dealt her, and feel bad for her. She had died by the time I returned to the UK, when I packed my bags and set off for Scotland to find my other family. But, nobody wanted to know about me, no one but Aunt Beth, who befriended me and told me about a past of which I knew nothing. Seeing the world into which I was born through my mother's eyes, courtesy of Aunt Beth's perspective, was an education. My mother, she said, was a meek and sensitive woman, a campaigner for the underdog. Frustrated into alcoholism, she had died young, in a fire.

My father, aware that he had left me without a mother, attempted to compensate for this imbalance by showering me with as much affection and spending as much time with me as possible. When he was not there, I was cared for by my aunts.

With his sound academic qualifications in mechanical engineering, my father worked as – I eventually did – in law enforcement, too; as a cop attached to the Vehicle Inspection Unit. From there he embarked on a meteoric rise to wealth and influence.

The entire Nigerian system, still intoxicated with the euphoria of independence, was one of wholesale grabbing. Few people could appreciate the magnitude of benefits that had been left for them by the departing British colonists, few could believe the power afforded to them now, few had been properly trained in the fine art of administration. Therefore, the immediate post-independence period saw the birth of the 'get rich quick' syndrome, which permeated every nook and corner of the young state.

My father, although basicallyan open and straightforward individual armed with the asset of European exposure, was sharp enough to take his own generous slice of the national cake. With an eye, too, for future security, he had the good sense to open doors for manyrelated kinsmen, and to make sound investments.

After a successful and silk-lined career, he died in 1987 of liver cancer, leaving behind a vast estate, from which his Familycould live comfortably till the end of their days. He left a legacy that placed his name a cut above any average Nigerian.

Despite the security and protection which I enjoyed as I grew up under the police umbrella, the comfort of readymade prosperity, the availability of sound education at reputable Nigerian schools, I seemed destined to become a casualty of the Nigerian corrupt system, which had become virtually institutionalised within a few years of independence. (Of course, ironically, this was years before the UK's system would ever learn of my name.)

As a young boy, I would reflect that it was from my mother that I inherited the innate instinct to rebel against injustice, not minding the odds against me. When you really look for it, injustice can be found in all manners of burrows and hideyholes – and I had a nose for sniffing it out, and grabbing the metaphorical bull by the horns to confront the issue at hand.

From an early age, most notably in my schooling career, this tendency began to manifest itself, drawing considerable comment from peers and adults alike.

Strong-arm tactics perpetually pitted me against bullies and though I often emerged second best, this did not dislodge my commitment to protecting the weak. My stubborn streak did not brook the negative; actually there was this instinctive disposition towards the benevolent facets of life. Doubtlessly a motivating factor was a Christian upbringing, fired with my father's firm disciplinary outlook. This was the kiln in which Michael Nsonwu was cooked and produced, before being unleashed on the world, as all children eventually are.

~

In the culture of stampede to loot the treasury in Nigeria after the departure of the British, the greater part of the indigenous population was not sufficiently well placed to take advantage, hence the birth of an unfair society in which morals had gone to the wind. To live in an unfair society was to witness the tremendous power of the irrational, which hung over the semblance of rationality. The end result was a dog-eat-dog society, with a complete disregard for the sanctity of human life.

From the frying pan of being culturally-outcast in Blantyre, to the fire of Nigeria's unfair instability; maybe this unhappy state of affairs could be taken for granted because of the Third World status of our industrial experience, and those who lived and breathed the system supposedly would not feel its destructive effects - except the drop-outs, borderline cases and foreign business tourists who would be exasperated by encountering exaction at every turn in life.

Even over time, I could not come to terms with the Nigerian system. I was never offensive or egotistical; it was stubbornness rooted in rebellion against anything which my instincts rejected as being innately wrong. My teachers could not tolerate it. Among my contemporaries, I was regarded as something of a 'softie.'

The unfair society of Nigeria was no place for me. The judges, lawyers, cops and warders were all in abundance, but there was next to no law enforcement. With sufficient funds, anybody could buy his way out of trouble. I almost preferred, in my wildest dreams, a reality where the trouble is fixed and inescapable, even if to my own detriment.

~

History tells us that matters in Nigeria degenerated to the level of crisis which prompted bloody military interventions and a protracted two and a half-year civil war; it surprised no one. Growing up in this system, up to the completion of my polytechnic education, took me beyond the civil war and into the era of oil boom, when the stampede of the get-rich-quick' syndrome turned into a raucous rugby scrum in which only the fittest could survive.

With no social welfare scheme to take care of the vast majority, who were falling by the wayside, I was ready to flee the country; jump back into the frying pan, so to speak. Return to my former home country, a land of my birth where I felt few roots and held fewer early memories. As I boarded a plane out of Nigeria, I recounted to myself my reasons for deserting - I did not like nepotism, I did not like tribalism, I did not like factional dissension, I did not like religious intolerance. These were the diabolical effects of an unfair society that had come into too much wealth.

~

It seemed ironic, somehow, that race relations was the one important area of social tolerance, notwithstanding Europe's oppressive colonial past in Africa and the occasional vexatious issues pertaining to unfavourable international politics on African affairs. The Caucasian was still subconsciously revered as some sort of visible god. While mixed marriages were generally frowned on, their progeny were embraced with open arms in Nigerian society.

In my own situation, the negative attitudes attached to taboo were mercifully checked by my father's influence and the attendant respect accorded him by our large extended family clan. My father on his part had demonstrated his stance with the deep affection he bestowed on me, which he ensured was noted by the world. He named me after himself.

I understood then, and know now, that my father felt he owed me a double responsibility and wanted to provide as much emotional and social protection as possible. Even when he married and was blessed with a further six children, he took steps to ensure there was parity in the treatment meted out to all his children. There was no such thing as favouritism or any act or word on his part that would create any basis for rivalry. He was fair, considerate and God-fearing to the last.

But he could not be everywhere; he could not know everything. The subtle undercurrents of rivalry were there. Those of the extended families who harboured resentment about my father's indiscretion knew how to display it without the need for words. The rash and fiery temperament of Nigerians, especially those of Ibo stock, was such that in any altercation on differing points of view, it was well nigh impossible that some bruising comment should not be made about my face. As such, it was well nigh impossible too, for complexes not to take root, branching out into suppressed annoyance during

moments of privacy.
While my father was ill, I kept my tears to myself. Personal grief tends to cloud one's sense of reason and dampens the enthusiasm to view the vicissitudes of life with the objectivity they demand. In such an instance, those elements of human behaviour which encouraged the negative, would come in for unmerciful and venomous cynicism.

Nigeria then became a pet hate, the deafening pandemonium created by the nation-wide scramble for wealth, with no rules governing the survival game, had the same irritant effect as a swarm of persistent flies drawn to the musky scent of human perspiration in the murderous heat. The Nigerian system instilled a deep yearning for law enforcement to be effected with a rod of iron. However, this severity would have to be measured with the kind of fairness, consideration and compassion that I imagined my unknown mother would have shown. *Where is she now? What was she really like?* I'll never fully know.

These people had not had two hundred years of industrial experience to evolve the self-discipline, responsibility and patriotic zeal required for creating the basis for a viable society. This is the Nigeria I know all too well.

The climate, too, played its part - the unforgivable African heat, which is like heat nowhere else in this world. Its intensity destroys sanity, prickling the skin and the senses; its humidity evaporating inside the skin and bringing on a weight of lethargy, sapping every ounce of strength from every joint and culminating in a dragging sense of something akin to zombiefication. Climbing the stairs is like tying tons of dead weight to your ankles, and the struggle to concentrate represents a punitive war against indecision and hopeless frustration.

Based on such experiences, one might think that I would find my future experiences with the prison system in the UK, and the attack at the hands of my co-workers, to be refreshingly normative. Alas, no. In fact, it was like being slapped with a wet fish; yet, one whose scent is all too familiar, and perhaps worse still, been left decaying in the sun, from a past long ago. I thought I had escaped these twisted cycles of injustice, these no-rules, no holds barred worlds, this scramble and pandemonium. How wrong I could be.

~

Given several millennia of hell-fire, it is easy to understand why the effects of the heat on the African is often misunderstood as monumental stupidity. And it is this misconceived stupidity that triggers and regulates the impetuous scramble for wealth at whatever cost, and damns the rules, that explains why the effort to establish a Western infrastructure in the African environment will proceed at a snail's pace. So, in this raucous bedlam of survival of the fittest, life is as haphazard as the plantings in farm allotments, back to front and upside down. Anything to shake off the searing heat and grab what is possible - enough hopefully - to purchase and install the air-conditioning that will invigorate the will, senses and limbs into some semblance of organised performance.

The European has an easy answer when caught in the hell of the African heat, he simply passes out.

The African people, then, could never be justifiably regarded as inferior to their Caucasian counterparts, nor less civilised by virtue of aeons-old cultural and migratory circumstances. Mechanisation can never be misunderstood for civilisation. Where racial tolerance prevails, it is applauded in the eyes of God because of its recognition of the sanctity and equality of every man. The European needs to learn some sound lessons about this area of sacred truth.

But still that is not to make excuses for the appalling savagery that characterised the

Nigerian way of life, and in the scenario of self centred callousness during the mindless scramble to amass wealth, most harrowing of all was the high-handed display of power by law enforcement agents as camouflage for underhand extortion from innocent laymen. Law is a powerful, intoxicating potion. The police had become the notorious predators of the people - criminals and law-abiding folks alike - their uniform the licence for nationalised gangsterism. As the police force was the most corrupt institution in Nigeria, where then was there room for law enforcement?

Somehow, notwithstanding the privileged protection that my family received from that institution, I shed no tears when my father retired from the force in 1975 to try his hand at private enterprise. But I was aware of feeling less protected now that he was an ordinary civilian, and was generally conscious of a sense of insecurity brought on by an oppressive system in which every man was a law unto himself.

In time, my father was handsomely rewarded by his flourishing steel production company, in which I participated full-time and earned my living until my departure to Britain in 1986.

In those intervening years, Nigeria gradually became the world's nightmare with the enduring scale of its corruption. But from one point of view there was no cause for despair: I had come to understand that the institutionalised chaos was not a reflection of some genetic inferiority in the make-up of a coloured person. It was a calculated ploy to facilitate the corruption culture. It provided effective camouflage for the wheelings and dealings to be perpetuated. The attendant snail's pace of officialdom was designed to invoke, and did invoke, a mandatory though unspoken provision for 'miscellaneous charges' in the profit margin; necessary if processes for payment were to be expedited. It was ingenious,

and it worked. But at what cost to the principle of law enforcement?

Slapping one hand to the forehead, I look back without fondness as justice was practically for sale in the courts, and the police, customs officers and prison warders serving as the law infringement scavengers among whose unofficial tasks was the duty of making returns to their overall bosses. The man in the street could hardly be expected to emerge as a saint of benevolent charm by comparison.

~

In the developing environment of kill or be killed, and divested of the cloak of protection by my father's retirement from the police force, I went for training in martial arts, gaining the satisfaction and confidence of seeing it work in occasional rough and tumbles with lawless desperadoes.

Military intervention in governance, far from providing the law and order claimed, only served to show up more glaringly the truism that the people of Nigeria were not yet ready for honest leadership. The 'do as

I say, not as I do' rule of military coercion inflicted on 'bloody civilians', saw punch-ups between soldiers and policemen in the streets. Above-the-law arrogance was displayed by half-witted and barely literate military hoodlums over the helpless and quaking subservient civil population – furthermore, in the face of licensed killers whose eligibility to rule the nation was a glorified nil.

At the end of the day, their greatest achievement was a scandalous plunder of the national treasury, in woeful perpetration of the corruption culture. And they were answerable to nobody.

Prayers became my sanctuary and refuge in the face of ubiquitous injustice in Nigerian society. It spurred me into hard, committed work in my father's company, and this helped to ward off depression about man's inhumanity to man.

There is a tendency for man to personalise his problems, focusing eagle eyes on his woes and bat eyes on the tribulations of mankind as a whole.

Similarly, there was the tendency to view the Nigerian milieu, oblivious to what happens in the rest of the world. The growing exodus of our 'brain drain', seeking greener pastures offshore, did not help matters. The compelling data from various schools of mass communication about the existing attractions of Western societies, and the visual evidence of the many Caucasians who thronged these shores for one mission or the other, only served to reinforce this trend.

Regardless, I belonged to the school of thought placing Nigeria on the top rung of the corruption ladder - and I wanted out. I could not bear to see hardship and in that regard, Nigeria was becoming a daily eyesore, which only law enforcement and justice could heal.

I was conscious too of something spiritual beckoning me away...

The British were my people as well, I reminded myself, so naturally I was drawn to be part of that scene. Would I fit in? Would I be better suited there? After all, my mother's blood also coursed through my veins. In my case, more than for my thoroughbred Nigerian contemporaries, Britain was the real 'Mother Country.'

Indeed, had I been familiar with the acute

observation of the late historian and essayist Philip Guedella, I would have been more drawn to my mother's native Scotland. "An Englishman is a man, who lives on an island in the North Sea, governed by Scotsmen."

I left for Britain in 1986, and as if satisfied that my future had been taken car of, my father died a year later. He had been forced to play the game the way the cards fell, to ensure future security for his family, but he had played that game with as much deference to the conscience as was possible in the circumstances.

I breezed in from my London base - where I was selling kitchens for Magnet, making a new life for myself - to contribute my tears to a befitting send-off for my father, and left a pledge to continue in the family tradition of law enforcement. Essentially that had been my sole preoccupation in life since reaching the age of reason.

1986 was another important year world-wide for conscientious rebellion and the principle of law enforcement:

A coup in Uganda toppled the government and Yoweri Museveni was declared the new President.

President Jean-Claude 'Baby Doc' Duvalier of Haiti resigned aged only 34, and took sanctuary in France.

In the Soviet Union, political prisoners, including Anatoly Scharansky and Yuri Orlov, were released and allowed to leave the country, an important stage in Gorbachev's liberalisation programme.

In South Africa, police fired on peaceful African demonstrators, killing 30 people.

American fighter planes attacked Gaddafi's headquarters in Tripoli; reprisal for Libyan involvement in terrorist activities against U.S citizens in Europe. The controversial attack resulted in a death-toll of fifteen civilians and triggered the retaliatory killings of three U.S. hostages in Lebanon.

Meanwhile, Michael Nsonwu flew to London Heathrow Airport at the age of 27, to embark on a future career of peace-making in a society that was reputed to be the most stable and civilised in the world.

~

As I entered the comparative silence of the

disembarkation hallway - in striking contrast against the uproarious Lagos airport scene - I was confronted with a tight-lipped police officer at every turn. Each time, the dark uniform and matching helmet materialised on the long walk to Immigration Control, I was reminded that the stability of the British state was rooted firmly in the rule of law, and that the police were always available to enforce that rule.

I was impressed but also overawed by the culture of silence. Nothing sums up more succinctly this peculiar attribute. Silence - a conversation with an Englishman! That silence reflecting the secret of the unique methodical organisation expected of a great people whose empire spanned over half the world. And in the silence of those police officers, I imagined I could discern a most perfect expression of scorn for the conscientious rebelliousness against injustice which I represented.

Notwithstanding the negative impressions of her notorious colonial past, and the recurring instances of racial prejudice that continued to besmirch her saintly record of human rights, justice and peace, Britain appeared to tower above all the other European groups in refinement and civilised conduct. Maybe this euphoric inspiration was rooted in a *bona fide* sense of belonging, birthright.

I was awed, I was thrilled, I looked forward to new experiences and challenges.

The future seemed bright and clear.

Chapter Three

"We have just enough religion to make us hate, but not enough to make us love one another."

~ Jonathan Swift

To the Nigerian who has fled from his homeland to the greener pastures of Britain, anticipating uninterrupted electric power supply, a constant supply of hot and cold tap water, a welfare system guaranteeing shelter and food for the impecunious and improvident citizen who finds himself forced below subsistence level - the list of privileges that distinguishes the UK as a true ready-made paradise is endless. The city lights of London are like clustered beacons of hope to the citizens of the world, who throng to them like so many mesmerised moths.

I was one of those moths with anticipations and dreams. And with these hopes and aspirations comes a distinct fragility, too; like the moth whose wings disintegrate with a human touch – as I shortly discovered upon the trying ordeal of a horrifying interrogation for a crime I didn't commit, and much later when I crossed paths with poor Lumumber (R.I.P.), as I will come to momentarily...

Though, certainly, I was tougher skinned than any moth, I was putting my life in the hands of a new system, with so much promise and relief on the horizon.

Yes, relief. There is such an overwhelming sense of relief to be able to walk along immaculate well-paved streets and try to shake off memories of the dusty unpaved streets of Lagos and accompanying heaps of filth and open drains. There is the intoxicating reality of a culture of absolute peace for the peaceful-minded, with its round-the-clock emergency services ready like coiled springs to answer distress calls in whatever shape or form with unfailing promptness.

I liked the idea of becoming part of that security in the UK, as my father had provided before me, back in Nigeria. However, the differences between the two countries didn't stop there. The natives had their differences, also. The thoroughbred Briton treasures quietude, privacy, and a strict minding of his own business - in contrast with the raucous, back-clapping laughter of attention-seeking Nosy Parkers in Nigeria.

As a native of both countries, so to speak, the product of a Nigerian father and Scottish mother; I bridged a gap and could unite the two in a common aim of locking away those who deserve to be punished. Or so I thought, idealistically perhaps, before contemplating those in the cells before me, their crimes, their sentences, and the 'monsters' that emerged at the other end of this machinery, to walk once more on these immaculately paved streets that are supposedly safe and sound.

~

When I first arrived into this wonderful environment of basic euphoria and contentment, I had the free reign to gather body and soul together in a way that would not have been possible back at home.

I had already come on a wing and a prayer from a culture of great spiritual worship. Yet, I discovered that abundant facilities and countless opportunities effectively sideline the significance of worship. The materialism, the necessity to perform, succeed and save up, under the aloof gaze of natives who have no tolerance for laziness and ineptitude, all serve as a reminder to the British people that religion is in the heart and not in the knees. Inadvertently the immigrant soon becomes afflicted with the same nonchalant indifference against the God who answered his prayers back home and brought him here in the first place!

Only when one attempts to merge into the anonymity of labour with folks of all creeds and colour will he begin to understand why it was the view of Napoleon Bonaparte that, "Religion is what keeps the poor from murdering the rich." The black worm may still breathe the same clean, crispy air, be catapulted into keen labour by the same invigorating chill, and feed well from the same fat of the land, but wherever he turns he will always be subtly reminded that he is still a black worm - or a poor worm of any colour, for that matter.

Only at that point of 'diplomatic awakening' would the Nigerian immigrant be compelled to continue believing in Christianity the way he believed in the sunshine of Africa - not only because he could see it, but because by it he sees everything else (I say in homage to C.S. Lewis). In this case, he sees the reality of his position in society when he looks down to see the bottom of the ladder on which he stands.

~

After two years of living in Britain, I was fortunate not to allow my faith in God to falter. But the reality of the colour-caste system in which I found myself can be summed up by this famous antiquated rhyme (which, nevertheless, still seemed to affect my socialization in the UK):

If you're white, you're right
If you're brown, hang around
If you're black, get back

I was more a shade of brown and elected to hang around, mainly, with fellow browns and blacks belonging to the working class and underprivileged brackets of society, and not with many whites at all. I was satisfied that the whites had no monopoly on righteousness. I was ready to assert my rights in this regard whenever the need arose, but always took steps to ensure I was never the aggressor.

Not that I was in any way underprivileged myself, far from it, but instinctively from infancy, I was drawn to the underdog; identified with his cause and fought his battles. I was sympathetic to hardship, and in this regard was generous to a fault to my friends who were most in need. Because I was always available with an attentive and compassionate ear, I became a magnet to many, never failing to provide succour and wise counsel.

Above all I was accessible, and forthcoming with companionship and inspiration. My passion for the 'liquorice-all-sorts; confectionery was a coincidental reflection of the types of friends I hung out with - loafers, good-time guys, fly-by-night merchants, compulsive gamblers, self-employed entrepreneurs, casual workers, civil servants, a few drug-addicts, a handful of well-to-do business men, and likeable nutcases.

Many of them were problem cases and our invaluable associations gave me privileged insight into many facets of human nature with the common problem of feeling hard-done-by in a system that was supposed to be the fairest and most stable in the world.

In the early days of my arrival, I meandered in and out of several job opportunities in London, all connected with security one way or the other; either as a security officer or an all-night officer. You could say I was rooted in some spiritual search to be part and parcel of effective law enforcement - in spite of my misgivings about the aesthetic drift of the British ruling class.

Still, I was ultimately unable to find the job satisfaction I craved. I wanted to be in the system, in a government position where I would be able to serve God by being my brother's keeper. Most social ills called for simple understanding and humane communication, and most victims were denied these.

I believed that if I was given a chance to relate with the human race in the same way as I interacted with my wide circle of friends, given the ease with which I could attract goodwill and comradeship, I could well have a future as a social worker. If the worst came to the worst, I mused in jest, I could join the clergy - whichever way it is looked at, I would be fighting injustice.

As irony would have it, it was through injustice that the final opportunity to pursue my cherished ambition came. One of my friends who might have been tagged with the label of 'dubious character' by less tolerant observers, somehow lived up to that unsavoury image when he was involved in some fraud that saw a large cheque being paid into my bank account. The police subsequently arrested me - or would it be more correct to say that I was coerced into going down to the station to answer some questions. This was the first time in my life that I had been involved with the police in a negative way that cast aspersions on my integrity; the shock was devastating.

The hostile and intimidating approach of my interrogators almost frightened me to death, as it had me believing I was about to be read my rights and charged with some criminal mischief of which I knew absolutely nothing. But they were merely playing on a hunch; engaged in psychological warfare to ascertain if I might be coerced into breaking down and spilling the beans. My protestations of innocence, my insistence that I was myself the victim of unscrupulous elements fell on sceptical ears.

It was only when they claimed, "You do realise, don't you, that we will get you sent back to Nigeria?" that I understood that they had misjudged my awareness of my own rights. They thought they were dealing with someone who did not know these things and could be pushed around.

"The hell you will!" was my defiant answer. "With my British passport?"

At this point, they told me I was free to go, but that I might be called back for further questioning. I gave a mental 'V' sign to my captors.

Overall, the incident left me in a bad state of nerves, and underlined the need to be more circumspect in my choice of friends. I was more conscious than ever before of the need to be properly protected in life, and the only effective protection lay in the law enforcement system itself.

That was not to happen until 1990 - surely one of the most auspicious years in the history of time for the triumph of justice and law enforcement on a global scale:

Dear old Nelson Mandela was released from prison near Cape Town at the age of 71, and President de Klerk sought his assistance to negotiate a political settlement between the Blacks and Whites.

The Lithuanians seceded from the Soviet Union. Deploring their action, Gorbachev sent tanks into Villius and cut off their oil supplies.

The East Germans held their first free elections since 1932.

Iraqi forces invaded Kuwait after she refused to comply with Saddam Hussein's demands to pay compensation for drilling oil on a tract of land allegedly belonging to Iraq and cede that disputed land to Iraq; twelve Arab and several European countries denounced Saddam's action, while the United Nations Security Council voted for economic sanctions against Iraq.

The world witnessed the joining of West and East Germany after 43 years of division, the unification having been approved in Ottawa by France, Britain, America and the Soviet Union.

The UN Security Council voted to authorise the use of military force to oust Iraq forces from Kuwait if they were still there after 15 January 1991.

And on 18 June 1990, the Principal Establishment Officer of Her Majesty's Prison Service Headquarters, South West London, was pleased to offer Michael O. Nsonwu an appointment as an established prison officer.

I had landed at last. It was gratifying to say the least, that I was not alone in my conviction of my ability to help my fellow men become better individuals and effect their rehabilitation.

The host of interview sessions, training courses and probationary period that preceded my final posting to Pentonville in September 1990 were all unanimously endorsed by the various authorities with the same assessment rating 'acceptable.' This thread of accord was a tribute to the high calibre of men who administered Britain's prison service!

Initial attachment reports at Pentonville credited me with being a "very smart well presented young man, confident, quite bright, answers showed a common sense attitude. Aware of problems he could face as a member of ethnic minority, has an equable temperament which should handle problems well. Father was Senior

Police Officer - appreciates disciplined way of life. Used to supervising staff as a controller in security."

I was struck by the tactful hint made by this particular interviewing chairman with regard to areas of possible discord on the grounds of race. I could never regard myself as being from any minority in the face of my spiritual outlook of being one with God in the majority.

While it was only realistic to recognise the need for some sort of rapport with those who provided the butter to the bread, there was an interesting consideration which called for caution -- the sparkling extrovert temperament of the Nigerian mirrors the sun-spangled climatic condition that gives rise to his warm, outgoing nature. Conversely, the cold, introverted silence of the Briton reflects the chill of their climate. There being no universal means of measuring cultures, a fair and merciful God had compensated them for the bleak harshness of their uncompromising weather, a reward which propelled them into productive research and creativity for their survival. They, in their ignorant arrogance, puffed by the bounties of their colonial conquests, misunderstood this as innate superiority over non-Caucasian, perhaps. They adopted this attitude, having failed to observe there existed endless records of non-Caucasians, many even darker than charcoal, who had availed themselves of the academic opportunities in the west and had demonstrated excellence on par with their European counterparts.

I wanted to be surrounded by happiness

and laughter, and where possible to bring the same to lives of those who were being denied them for reasons beyond their control. The solemn demeanour of the Briton at home denotes seriousness and responsibility. To maintain and expand the luxuries gracious Providence brought their way, they were intolerant of any distraction from their workaholic ways. They sought a perfect finish and could not afford to make too many mistakes. There were negative side-effects however: neurosis; a significant lack of the human touch except where it related to improvement; love directed towards their creations and animals more than human beings; and where fellow mortals failed to display any aptitude for imaginative flair, there was at best diplomatic condescension, at worst outright contempt - well hidden behind diplomatic deception based on respect for public opinion. As I matured and became more spiritually aware, I came to realise that rather than the behaviour being premeditated, it was a result of materialism and a sense of separation.

I had no time in my life for such attitudes, but was willing to tolerate them only in as much as the authorities of the host country called the shots. But such compromise as I would be compelled to make would never lead me to abandon the ideal remedy - as advocated by the late Spanish philosopher and poet Shem-Tob Falaquera, for pretence he advised:

Adapt yourself to time and circumstance, So will you be untroubled every day If you meet a lion – Roar
But if you meet an ass, just bray.

That became my guiding principle in life. And that was the only way for a person of colour to survive in British society.

People like the less tolerant old papa who was disputing my place in a post office queue and could not resist the urge to throw in the slur, "Why not go back to your own country and do some good, why come here and be abstract?" was silenced with the most unprintable torrent of verbal communications he had ever heard in his life.

Similarly, the leader of a gang of drunken white youths challenging me with a broken bottle near a block of council flats in North London, was immediately confronted with the long needle of a geometry compass which I happened to be carrying on me, and made to understand that this would be plunged direct into his heart. We became friends thereafter.

But prison work was a different kettle of fish. It was dangerous. The three month preparatory training involved a course in unarmed combat to extricate oneself from the very real physical dangers inherent in prison work. But, with any amount of training, it truly took certain types of people to be 'complete' prison officers. The unanimous verdict of myself from some dozen interview session was 'acceptable.' Which meant there might have been some applicants who made the grades 'good' and 'very good' just as there were no doubt some who were regarded 'not acceptable' and 'totally unsuitable.'

While these interviewing authorities were essentially shrewd judges of men, because they were not spiritual (or did not appear to be, at any rate), I was confident that they had misjudged my full capabilities. But then, they were not to know that there existed an intangible spiritual link, which would predispose me to good human relations.

In some ways, I was born to be in this line of work. My temperament suited it. My personality craved it. And my background and experiences pointed to it. It was so clear now that I belonged here, even if others would one day disagree so vehemently that I would be beaten till half dead. Not 100% dead, like Lumumber. His belonging was opposed so strongly that he would never breathe again. Although I agree that he didn't

belong at Pentonville, my choice would

have been to free the man; an innocent man.

~

This needs to be said because on settling into prison work, something of a revolution took place at Pentonville prison with regard to inmate/officer relationships. My record in dealing with inmates proved to be far better than merely 'acceptable' and throughout my career at Pentonville, I deepened this with the power of regular contemplation and meditation. Old fashioned and soft maybe, but remarkably effective. As George Michael aptly stated, "You've got to have faith."

In fact, when assigned to the 'unconvicted' wing in the initial stages of my training, it was clear that this spiritual element underscored my early successes. The training officers could only explain away this potential to do well to mere feeling.

One of my report cards noted: “Of smart appearance, can express himself well and has a sense of humour. Has completed his first two weeks satisfactorily. But one feels he has the ability to achieve higher standards if only he will make the effort.”

Fortunately, there followed a more glowing and enthusiastic report from another experienced training officer: “He is able to control inmates, establishes good relationships with inmates and helps where possible. Does so to a good standard. Maintains a humanitarian approach within the context of fair and fair discipline. Mixes well with colleagues and senior staff. A well-turned out man who I feel will maintain the high standard he has set for himself. Has had no late recorded against him and only one day's sick."

The final testimonial, just six months later, which made me eligible for the 'convicted' wing, complimented me as being: "A hard working officer who is not frightened to seek advice from more experienced staff. Deals well with the day to day pressures on the unconvicted wing and can be quite tactful when required. A promising start to his career."

Maybe I was too occupied in trying to toe the line and make a good impression to question the principle of confining inmates who had not been convicted of any wrong doing in a court of law. But I appreciated that their potential to turn into hardened criminals who could constitute a danger to society necessitated their protective detention to save them both from themselves and the human population. Seen in the light of a humane policy of rehabilitation and help, and being 'screened' away from the more stringent corrective purification process being applied on their convicted neighbours, it seemed right and fitting.

However, what enhanced my early success considerably, and made life in Pentonville so much easier, was the tumultuous outpouring of emotions all over the world on the release of Nelson Mandela. It gave the greatest inspiration to the black inmate majority to witness the unruffled calm and dignity of the man. It seemed to confirm that there was some dignity in spending time in jail and coming out a gallant hero. The event was like a counselling in itself. Sometime later, when Mandela's career would be documented on television and riveting glimpses of the notorious Rhobben Island prison offered to viewers. The inmates of Pentonville well appreciated the comparative luxury they were experiencing. I went out of my way to open the eyes of some of the juvenile inmates to this fact - Mandela was someone to emulate. It was a successful approach to counselling and rehabilitation in the sense that having established my close rapport with inmates, resulting in a very natural exchange of dialogue and trust. It was a follow-the-leader type of appreciation.

When asked in one of my interviews to describe the qualities a prison officer should possess, my answer was: "He should be sympathetic, courageous, understanding and determined." I made sure that my duties were carried out according to these qualities, using good sense, good judgement, maturity and conscientiousness to be my brother's keeper.

Everything appeared to be going smoothly, all the way into the middle of 1991, by which time I had totally absorbed the frenetic rhythm of prison life and had perfected the art of bringing a smile to the lips of even the most manic depressive inmates - while attracting scowls of envy across the features of his colleagues. Prayer and meditation were the name of the game, and it was a great achievement to have been able to convert some of the inmates to this realm of human sanity.

Then, as if rising up to my challenge

against evil, fate started to play more discordant notes. I had just returned from lunch, and the order came to unlock the cells for recreational activities. While we were hurrying the inmates to get on with their various activities, I received a message from the SO (Senior Officer) to go and fetch a 'body' (prison slang for transfer) from B wing. I found this a source of relief, as it spared me the drudgery of nannying adults while they played their games.

Stepping into the huge corridors of B wing (this wing was the largest in European prisons), I caught sight of a familiar figure. I gaped in disbelief at my friend from childhood, Edward. Just the weekend before I had been with him, and could not believe he was in 'blues' (convicted inmates wore blue uniforms). I was flabbergasted to say the least, I had not even been aware that he had a case against him, let alone a conviction! I watched him as he darted into a cell on the 'Two's.' I hurried into an office and quickly tapped his name into the computer. Sure enough there he was. Details of his conviction spilled out on the screen. An involuntary whistle escaped my lips as I looked at his file, which showed a list the length of my arm. However, this was his first custodial sentence.

Every personal instinct inside me rebelled at this reality. Edward was someone for whom I would always have vouched without qualm.

I noted his location, and went back to my wing. "What a bloody mess!" I thought out loud as I sat down alone in the staff room.

Edward and I both grew up in Nigeria. It was not so much the crime of fraud that horrified me, but the record of so many previous suspended sentences and fines - of which I was in total ignorance. He was someone who was like my own brother.

After the evening lock-up, I went to his cell and unlocked the door. He looked up at me and smiled. "It may seem a silly question, but what on earth are you doing in here?" I asked as calmly as I could in our native lingua franca, Ibo

"Not surprised to see you, Michael. Know you work here and anyway I saw you earlier."
"Answer me, what are you doing here?"
"I've been framed, Michael."
"Knock off lying. I've seen your files."
He shrugged. "Have you got a cigarette?"

I handed him my packet, he took one, lit it and puffed and exhaled freely.
"You could do business if you smuggle in some stuff," he suggested. "Some items sell for ten times the street value, you must know that."

Warning bells sounded in my mind. "You could put me in trouble. I've got to leave. We'll discuss it again tomorrow."

I left his cell with my mind in a whirl; it was official prison service policy that if you were related to an inmate or knew him socially, you had a duty to report it, as there was the danger of your professionalism being compromised. For me, inclination and duty became locked in a stalemate. Inclination tempted me to protect my close friend, keep quiet about our friendship. Duty reminded me of my loyalty to my employers. It took three days of prayers and anxious thought.

When I told my Senior Officer the whole story, he advised me to put in an official memo requesting my friend's transfer. When I had done so, I went down to the allocation unit and explained the situation to the staff. They promised to send Edward to a comfortable nick. Wryly I wondered whether such a place exists anywhere in the world.

To this day, Edward harbours grudges against me over that incident; true friendship is never serene.

But if that episode left a sour taste in my mouth, the tumult that hit me just a month or two later turned me into the kind of person I would never have imagined I could become. Maybe that was how God wanted it, maybe if it had not happened I would have gone through life with rose-tinted spectacles, never able to gain a clear picture of what truth was all about.

~

The day started like most routine days. We had just finished serving breakfast and all the inmates had been 'banged up' before the beginning of normal daily activities.

I noticed that one of the cell lights was on (indicating assistance required). Unlocking the door, I challenged the inmate: "Yes, mate?"
"Open door, man. Me go home," he called, gesticulating. He was built like an ox.
"Where are you from?"
"Zaire."

"What are you doing here?"

"I came to Britain, need political asylum, persecution back home. Why being detained, no understand."

"What's your name?"

"Lumumber."

"Lumumber? I remember that name. Lumumber of the Belgian Congo. He towered as one of the icons of the struggle for African independence. He was assassinated in the Sixties for his political stand and socialist beliefs, wasn't he?"

Lumumber nodded. "Help me?"

"I'll see what I can find out."

"Thanks, man."

I made some basic checks, then returned to his cell and gently explained, "I'm afraid that you are an illegal immigrant, and because the detention centres are full, the authorities have decided to bring some of those charged under the Immigration Act to our remand wing. I advise you to go for your association, your landing is on association. I promise I will telephone the Immigration Department about your case."

He seemed puzzled. I repeated the words slowly. "Thanks, man - appreciated. Very kind." With that I let him out of his cell and went about my morning duties.

When I returned to the wing some forty-five minutes later, Lumumber was by the gates.
"Hey, what are you doing here?" I asked him
"Open gate, me go home!" he said forcefully.
I put my arm around his shoulder. "Come on, we will go and talk about it."
He followed me, protesting, "No need to

talk. Me innocent, me go home."

We had barely taken ten steps when suddenly, from the base wing, up rushed six officers. They were fully clad in anti-riot gear. Unbeknownst to me, an officer had earlier - in English - given Lumumber a direct order to leave the wing gates. But French was his second language, and I'd already discovered his English was limited.

The next few seconds were a blur. Lumumber frowned in confusion. I waved my hand and shook my head as the officers advanced, batons raised...
"Lumumber speaks French, there's been a communication problem," I intervened.
"Let me escort him back to his cell."

"Step aside," was the gruff reply. "He's

already refused a direct order."

"I don't suppose he understood," I tried to reason with them.

In a flash, they jumped on the unarmed prisoner – Lumumber was large, at 6 foot 3 inches tall, and bubbling with life, he seemed formidable, but not so formidable as to resist six officers to restrain him. They wrestled Lumumber to the ground quickly, and applied locks on his wrists. Frightened and bewildered, Lumumber started to struggle, but as there were six of them it was futile. I watched helplessly as he was dragged downstairs to the 'block,' which comprised of specially-constructed cells for recalcitrant inmates.

As I was catching my breath and controlling my emotions, I had a fleeting image of Lumumber in my mind's eye – he looked sorry and broken as they lugged him away. Five minutes later, there was a flurry of movement as we were told to lock up all the inmates. It later transpired that Lumumber was dead.

I was stunned; I could not believe it. I ran into the office to confirm what I had just heard. "You ignorant buffoons," I screamed at the top of my lungs. "You've killed him! You've killed him!"

In the principal officer's office, one of my superiors tried to calm me down. I was numb with shock, a whirlwind of emotion tearing me apart. There was guilt: maybe, if I had not let him out for association, he would still be alive. There was profound sorrow: at the way ignorance of different cultures could result in such a tragedy.

There was anger: those murdering officers showed no remorse, concerned only about covering their tracks. There was hopelessness: as I listened to those involved in the tragic incident discuss how they would put up a united front. There was horror: at the banter and jokes as some officers suggested taking photographs with their legs on top of Lumumber, 'sick joke of a prize kill.'

All these emotions catalysed and a new Michael Nsonwu was born.

~

The whole issue of race came into a sharper, more realistic focus. Gone were the days of shrugging my shoulders and adopting a philosophical attitude to that explosive and destructive, that unfair hydra-headed monstrosity; racial prejudice.

Those officers who killed Lumumber were going to walk away free, and at great cost to the tax payer be allowed to continue their jobs as agents of justice - apparently wholly oblivious to the absurd hypocrisy.

A new circular instruction regarding Control and Restraint in UK prisons was issued to all prison officers in 1996 as a result of a 1993 inquest into Lumumber's death at Pentonville prison. The inquest jury found that Lumumber was unlawfully killed by the six officers who used "improper methods of excessive force." No disciplinary charges were ever brought against those responsible. Lumumber was aged 32.

This tragedy was to spell the beginning of my troubles with Her Majesty's Prison Service. Those troubles were rooted in my painful awakening to the reality that prisons are the most negative places in the physical world and I was living off their murky spoils.

Chapter Four

"He that will not reason is a bigot, he that cannot reason is a fool and he that dares not reason is a slave."

~ William Drummond

Those who stamp out injustice need big boots. And, indeed, they are big boots to fill – while, as a man raised in a home by a father in law enforcement, who would enter into a career in 'justice' myself; I felt even more since Lumumber's killing that this was an unjust atrocity left right at my doorstep.

"Injustice anywhere is like injustice everywhere," I believe Booker T. Washington once said. The literary sage's wisdom made sense to an ordinary layman like myself, and it rang true at this moment in my life. The moment when everything seemed totally 'All Screwed Up.'

The injustice meted out to Lumumber haunted me for longer than I care to remember, but ultimately I realised that no man can think clearly when his fists are clenched. When the clouds of anger were allowed to disperse by the demands of objectivity and rationality, it was on human beings in general that the dust of my cynicism settled.

By nature, my mind is analytical. Thus, analysing the murderous nature of my earlier rage, I had to wonder whether I would have felt any better if those prison officers responsible for Lumumber's death had been black. The implications of a racially motivated attack disturbed me, as a Nigerian immigrant to Britain. I wondered, as someone who is part of the system that took the life of an innocent man; would the immensity of his death have been reduced if the officers were of the same skin as him?

Yet, where in any penal system would it be appropriate for officers to gang-up on an unarmed prisoner? Certainly it would be difficult to imagine a situation where a group of exclusively black prison officers in a penal system administered by whites, in an essentially white country, would be assigned to handle a disobedient black inmate, and apply such coercion as to lead to his untimely death. I had never known it to happen at any rate, not in England. But, there had been several instances of deaths of white inmates resulting from violent struggles with white prison officers.

These could not be labeled 'racist.' So it could have been that being black was only *how* Lumumber died, as opposed to why he died.

Nevertheless, any amount of reasoning and postmortem analysis would provide little comfort or consolation. The law of the land did not view the matter of race in such simple, clear-cut-terms - maybe a way of throwing the scent off the lawmakers who were themselves found wanting in that regard. Maybe they're just blind or indifferent to the tragic effects and consequences of race relations gone awry.

Though, certainly, there is something intangible about discrimination on the grounds of race that dehumanizes its victims in a way that ordinary forms of prejudice do not. That is why the Race Act of 1976 [expanded by the Race Relations (Amendment) Act 2000] and the Race Relations Board exist; ostensibly outlawing such forms of injustice. That's the idea, anyways...

Truly, no such law protects any hapless victim of discrimination on account of say an outstanding paunch or an oversized head, colour of hair, or even religion. Legislation purports to prevent discrimination but when the good Lord is the only other party to have direct access into the thoughts of an individual, how can the aggrieved secure the proof which would provide him with redress in the challenge of showing the actual *mens rea* of an accomplished racist?

On this occasion, the secret inner-workings of the racist British establishment would have no cause to worry about exposure. Lumumber's death was incidentally tragic by virtue of the victim's colour and racial origins, inflamed even more incidentally by the Caucasian race of his killers. But, in the absence of concrete proof that there was a motivation to kill based on rigidly-held supremacist views, Lumumber's demise was apparently just unfortunate - just as the similar death of a white inmate in seemingly similar circumstances, whether at the hands of white or black prison officers, would also be unfortunate. I was satisfied that Lumumber's colour was a contributory factor to the degree of violence that resulted in his death.

Therefore, I harboured a bitterness over the incident and eventual verdict of misadventure. JP Morgan's philosophy seemed to sum everything up: "A man always has two reasons for doing anything, a good reason and the real reason."

~

"All say how hard it is that we have to die, a strange complaint to come from the mouths of people who have had to live" - Mark Twain.

To me, death is more universal than life; everybody dies, but not everybody lives. This is particularly true of prison inmates. Not withstanding the purifying effects intended from their confinement, its grim reality highlights a sad situation - fear of love.

In the first place, the absence of love was the underlying cause behind the circumstances that led to their imprisonment. I remember looking into the eyes of a loveless man, the day that serial killer Fred West arrived at Pentonville and I would be there at his preliminary interview. Being raised in an abusive environment, without any love, is what created this monster. His own death would be at his own hands, ultimately; found hanging in his cell on New Years Day. No love lost there.

But, to fear love amounts to a fear of life, and those who are afraid of life are already three-quarters dead.

The prison inmate really is the living dead. Emotionless, plodding along, dead inside. His case is the toughest challenge of survival. For him, love is like measles, all the worse when it comes late. But, for many an inmate it never came at all - a tragic situation in a society whose readymade structures are rooted in romantic love. Sometimes that situation can be a double-edged sword, especially when viewed through the eyes of thinker Fran Lebowitz, who said that "Romantic love is a mental illness, but it is a pleasurable one. It's a drug, it distorts reality, and that's the point of it. It would be impossible to fall in love with someone that you really saw."

That probably explains why the missionaries in Africa, with a message of romantic love in a culture where the absence of twilight also mirrored the absence of love, were largely successful in selling Christ to the people. Many black people came to share the experience of Henry Ward Beecher through the missionary's scripture of love: "I never knew how to worship until I knew how to love." But the snail's pace of Africa's industrial growth, which would otherwise have installed the kind of structures that would have enhanced a culture of love, was counterproductive, the very antithesis of love. This is best reflected in the African penal system, which served somehow to assuage my mourning for Lumumber when I reflected on the comparative torture that was the lot of the African inmate.

Compared to the mollycoddled British inmate, Nigerian prisons are a veritable Hell on Earth.

~

I was never (openly) good at hypocrisy. If I had been as vociferous as my pent-up emotions over the Lumumber affair screamed for, I was aware that one of my white colleagues, losing patience, would have flared: "Clean your finger before you point at my spots." And quite rightly, because should the spotlight of attention have been turned to the Nigerian penal system as it existed then and for the most part still exists, the killers of Lumumber would have emerged as saints of benevolent charm when compared to their counterparts in that hottest part of Hades.

A visit to the typical Nigerian prison is an assault on the senses, with its perennial reek of human waste, bespeaking hygienic conditions that would put a skunk to flight. With that and the murderous heat, without relief of cooling systems, you don't have to stretch your imagination to appreciate the true meaning of Hell. Such a horrific picture becomes clearer when the converted demons, who represent law enforcement therein, with their primitive and high-handed display of brutal and sadistic power, come into focus. Injustice of the nature that visited Lumumber has remained a commonplace occurrence for those recalcitrant inmates who refuse to accept the fact that, in a Nigerian prison, they have no rights!

It goes without saying, however, that the Nigerian inmate would have given anything to swap places with the living Lumumber, if only to be able to luxuriate in a depth of comfort that he would probably not experience in his motherland even as a free man: a dry room with a bed, running water, electricity, and shelter above his head, knowing where his meals are coming from...

The British penal system has sanitary conditions that are as good as public conveniences in the free society of England herself, let alone Africa. The cold climate in its essence is preservative, without the discolouration and decay that follow in the wake of arid clouds of dust and heat. Any filth likely to be visited on its surroundings has to come from man and his personal habits, which the disciplinary policies of the penal system set out to do away with. So in that condition of basic comfort, the British penal system has every kind of recreational facility on offer to keep body and soul together – even if being held within, against your will.

~

Let me take you on a journey to the other side. A tale of life behind bars for a typical Nigerian prisoner. The British prison might not be The Ritz, yet – firstly - in terms of amenities, a Nigerian is lucky if has football as about the only real outlet, while the British inmate is spoilt by comparison. At his disposal is a gym for all manner of keep-fit courses, as well as football, table-tennis, billiards, snooker, library, television, decent food and heating are all available, representing a culmination in ever-changing reforms across many years; all calculated to develop strategies of rehabilitation and corrective measures.

No wonder then that the British have always claimed their penal system to be the most civilised in the world.

By this rationale, the legacies left for their

former colonies should, but for their Third World status, have been on par with what happens in the Mother Country. However, when left in the charge of inadequately trained local authorities who could only behave true to type, especially with the departure of the colonial rulers; one is perpetually confronted with a pitiful picture of man's inhumanity to man, with the offenders drawing more sympathy than those whom they victimised.

The penal system in the colonies at the height of the British Empire highlighted the barbarity that occurred after their departure even more for what it was. A humane system of rehabilitation for offenders existed, involving the creation of community jobs and counseling. The psychological power wielded by the established authority of the Crown over the native subjects contributed in no small measure to making this system easily absorbable by both the African offenders and prison officers.

In those days, society witnessed the touching sight of imported discipline in the penal system, when up to a dozen uniformed inmates walked in pairs from the prison to cut grass in the residential gardens of eminent civil servants three miles away, shepherded by a single uniformed warder, armed with nothing more menacing than a truncheon, the badge of authority and occasional barks to move faster. There were no handcuffs or leg-cuffs to prevent resistance or escape, nor would such an idea remotely cross the minds of the inmates. They would walk along in an orderly, disciplined fashion; the way docile sheep would move under the authoritative programming of superior man. It denoted absolute psychological defeat by a system which, contrary to what they might understand, was bent on recognising the dignity of man through a

civilised approach of counseling and gentle guidance.

In the initial stages of such a novelty, it presented a bizarre spectacle to onlookers sprung from a culture in which the buying and selling of humans into slavery catered for the practice of slaves escaping from their captors if availed of an opening. Had some jinx been placed on these captives to deprive them of their own free will? And what was greater - the brutal savagery to which captives were customarily subjected or the ease with which they could be dispatched from life without repercussions from any higher authority? This contrasted sharply with the civilised treatment of these modern captives and the good health they radiated in detention.

For many Africans, the Colonial experience seemed full of contradictions as well as ironies. On the one hand, the colonist came in with their hefty firepower and in the course of their subjugation of the indigenous population, killed and wounded many, after which extreme ruthlessness was used to enforce subjugation. Yet, this repressive new system appeared bent on enforcing policies which recognised the sanctity of human life, respected the dignity and free will of man, wanting to create the basis for a viable society in which every man should be counseled in the correct approach to expressing his free will within the confines of law and order.

The system seemed committed to giving every miscreant a chance to be resettled, without prejudice to the appropriate dose of punishment being dispensed for flouting the law – as always, such punishment would never fail to recognise the pedestal atop of which rests the dignity of man.

Thus, it was with the advent of Colonial rule that the hitherto barbaric penal system of Africa was given the civilised touch, and actually served to instill in the minds of the native population the impression of the whole man as a kindly and loving human-god. That was why the seemingly unlikely situation of a dozen unchained inmates being shepherded along by one scarcely-armed warder as if they had no minds of their own, was indeed a stark reality. They even preferred to chant hymns while cutting the grass in designated areas with cutlasses that they could so easily use to overpower the one truncheon-armed officer and flee then to entertain any negative thoughts in that direction.

Despite the apparent simplicity of escape, the British Empire in Africa gave birth to model prisoners. Doubtless a contributory factor to this was the accompanying missionary venture, which saw global love and worship of the Christian God at its height. Preaching the aforementioned romantic principles of love and forgiveness, and championed and patronised by the Colonial headquarters in London; the message of Christ would have seemed inappropriate if criminal offenders were denied their anointed share from the divine brush of mercy. Moreover, with their comparatively unenlightened minds, they were easily susceptible to the fire and brimstone denunciations against sin, hence making life for the prison governors and the society at large, much easier.

If I might continue my impromptu history lesson: When the British left Nigeria, matters reverted to the original format of eye-for-an-eye brutalities against criminals. In the rural communities, crime was punishable by slave-like incarceration, horrendous tortures, and ritualised capital punishments that would have made the Stone Ages seem like an aristocratic tea party by comparison; working side-by-side with more modern penal procedures in urban communities. What was so modern about those procedures anyway? Prison authorities grew fat through blackmailing the dependants of inmates, sometimes masterminding murder or serious maiming of inmates in the face of non-compliance, regardless of what excuses the families may have given for not finding the money to pay.

The injustice of the system was even more glaring against the hypocrisy of institutionalised criminality, which characterised Nigeria's get-rich-quick syndrome, evidently intended to catch and punish small fry, while leaving the monopoly of big-time thievery to those manning the key positions of power. Certainly, Nigeria became a boiling cauldron of criminality, and because the government of the day led by example in this regard, it became well nigh impossible to prevent the consequent birth of a new culture that overwhelmingly recognised the virtue of outwitting and cheating as representing individual talent - just don't call it crime, that's all.

No, real criminals were those incompetent enough to get caught, and their branding and exclusion from mainstream society served to create a sub-culture; a them-and-us situation that acted as fodder for feeding more crime.

In Nigeria and other African cultures where this approach was extreme, death penalties by firing squads and public hangings before cheering crowds merely served to harden offenders. This often resulted in victims being eliminated by criminals, in order for them to escape identification, in the knowledge that capture meant death.

In the light of these facts, one might cry to

the British, "Come back, all is forgiven!" But only concerning the saintly penal system that colonialism introduced to Nigeria. Instead of hardening offenders and turning them into monsters, the system practised a more humane policy of making offenders feel responsible by recognising the iniquitous nature of their crimes against God. The British penal system as it existed then created the awareness that, for as long as one failed to address the issue of responsibility, then one would inadvertently fail to correct these social anomalies.

But, the Nigerian penal system that replaced it in the wake of independence did the exact reverse. One could make out a genuine case for forgiveness to God, considering that the black man was cursed with the lethargic effects of the heat, spoiled by the abundance of fruits and crops with which to grow fat and lazy and comparativelyunproductive. Without the commensurate get-up-and-go creative flair with which the cold weather compensated those natives denied the free luxuries, fertility of soil and abundant natural resources; the African people were dead-weights in the energy-sapping heat of their climate. In conclusion: laid-back, dull of mind, bereft of rational and creative thought, primitive, instinctive, intuitive and spiritual, without the mind to evolve a culture of exploration of the material world around them, let alone to go out and conquer other distant lands and peoples they could not have imagined existed.

While the basics of education and knowledge availed them through the colonial process now made it possible for them to be enjoying the mechanised fruits of their own natural resources in the modern age, the very fact of the rudimentary status of their experience in the quest for scientific knowledge (as deliberately designed and programmed by the super powers calling the shots off-shore) ensures that in terms of almost everything - from architecture, infrastructure, culture, wealth and definitions of right and wrong - their way of life will remain of a lower quality than that in the developed world. That's the facts, as I see them...

And so, the African inmate continues to be dehumanised, marginalised, hardened and anything but reformed, resulting in a boomerang effect that will serve to further criminalise an already unfair society.

Meanwhile, the British penal system,

operating under an institutionalised policy of continuous improvement for the lives of the native British people, would be seeking ways of providing more comfort for its prison inmates within a basic corrective design. Ostensibly then, the Africans are retrogressing into further barbarity while their polished neo-colonialists are growing more refined in their treatment of their fellow human beings.

It's a grim state of affairs, especially if you are the prisoner serving the same time, for the same crime, in very different standards/countries.

~

Reflecting on these realities in relation to the killing of Lumumber; all I could feel was screwed-up. To engage in undue condemnation of both his killing and the British penal system was to indulge in double talk, double standards. There were so many more Lumumber-type killings in Nigerian prisons - no less painful because the perpetrators were black but, at any rate, they were oft carried out without any reasoning of race or ethnic or tribal origin, nor for being a shade lighter or darker in skin colour.

Without a doubt such causes, had they motivated the killings, would - to the outside world - have made the deaths more outrageous, more scandalous, more painful, more tragic, than any other reason. Which is to say that, by human standards, race prejudice does indeed dehumanise its victims in a way that ordinary forms of prejudice do not. Still, that does not excuse the gravity of unwarranted killing for whatever other reason.

But, my point is this - in looking at the barbarity of the Nigerian penal system when compared to the contrasting humanity of its British counterpart, one is still confronted with the issue of race and colour prejudice at the end of the day. It is not by choice that the prison officers of the Nigerian penal system have remained comparatively backward and unlettered. Circumstances over which they had no control prevailed to ensure that their level of exposure remained basically rudimentary in order to maintain the social order in favour of the Caucasian stock. It would indeed be regarded as disastrous to the social order if the reputedly 'inferior' black men were availed of opportunities that would enable them to become on par with their former colonists and slave-masters. And, human talent having no bounds, one could never rule out the possibility of a take-over of the balance of world power by the black race. Hence the seemingly endless oppression of the black man, on a scale that ensured his permanent back-seat position, even in his own country.

~

Every black African nation is virtually amenable to the discipline of Whitehall, Paris or Washington; and any radical or Marxist-inclined 'independent' nation ultimately finds itself saddled with economic crisis that precipitates a 'brain drain' plague. This in turn leaves the reins of government power in the hands of unlettered mediocrity that will preside over poverty and corruption.

It is racism all the way. The unwitting victims of this subtle European manipulation are, in their essence, people of goodwill making the best of situations thrust upon them by evil, to the best of their limited understanding. They mean no harm by virtue of their inability to speak and appreciate the Queen's English in a way that would be acceptable by British standards. They mean no harm in driving at break-neck speed along a crowded High Street. They mean no evil in not having been privileged with exposure to the niceties of hygiene, etiquette, law-abidance, and other such essentials of human survival. They mean no harm that their policy is largely one of drift and they do not really know their own minds. They may be forgiven for their lackadaisical manner and the slow, languid movements of their gait instead of the brisk purposeful walk of the native British.

Likewise, it is only in accordance with their level of understanding that their application of power against such victims as prison inmates attracts the label 'barbaric' to the developed world, while to them it is right and fitting. They are not motivated by logic, sometimes doing the most extraordinary things and finding it difficult to explain why they do them. They mean no harm by this unfortunate failing. So these African law enforcers are as much unfortunate victims of the system under which they operate as the victims of their style of law-enforcement, unwittingly battling against an ultimate off-shore power that despises their squalor yet at the same time would loathe a situation where they are able to rise above it. In the same vein that offshore power will secretly encourage the brutalities meted out against fellow African countrymen in the name of law-enforcement, and at the same time castigate such coercion in the Western media as human rights abuse.

Exactly the same motive was intended and achieved by the British Government's invitation after the war to citizens of the Caribbean islands. They were invited to come to 'Mother Country' to engage in menial tasks, which the native British considered beneath their dignity to touch. They responded to the call in droves, only to be told at the end of the day that they constituted an 'Immigrant Problem' and should now go back home! Such a vicious circle has been the lot of blacks the world over, enslaving their potential and restricting their free will - and in the case of corrupt, poverty stricken repressive systems in Africa, no marks for guessing where the dredges of mediocrity who throng the corridors of power lodge, for safe-keeping, the looted monies granted as lifelines from European 'philanthropy' (European banks!) while their ailing economies become further indebted to European creditors for the entirety of the original loans.

But, unfortunately for Her Majesty's Prison Service, I did not proverbially slip through these institutional cracks into the pre-assigned pigeon-holes presented to me; the Britain I emigrated to, the penal system that employed me, perhaps would not understand how such a well-read and intelligent Nigerian man could come to be, let alone be here and drawing these simple conclusions about this country and pondering such thoughts of their long history in Africa and subsequent developments...

Although, in reality, it is not difficult to appreciate that the British penal system falls into two distinct categories:

1) The home system that caters for a policy of continuous improvement in the welfare and corrective measures being applied to the inmates, within the framework of improving comfort and civilising influence expected of a major industrial power.

2) The retention of the barbaric and retrogressive denial of human rights against inmates of the former colonies, corresponding with the generally

unhealthyeffects of crude despotic governance, thus creating a boomerang cycle of negative chain-events which will serve to warp the potentials of the people as a whole!

And even on the home front, while the corrective measures and improvement sought for British inmates in an atmosphere of relative comfort were being applied - for those of ebony hue, just fortunate enough to latch on to a good thing, the British System had its subtle ways of reminding them that they are different and inferior – but, try proving it. You can't because racial bias is so often lurking in the mind, and rarely worn on a sleeve, except in the ramblings revealed at the pub with close cohorts.

Oh well - whichever way it is looked at, no

matter how well camouflaged behind diplomatic conjuring tricks, the British system caters for a policy of racism both at home and abroad, in my experience this is the case. The policymakers of the British establishment find it easy to protect obnoxious policies that enforce white supremacy policies behind the Official Secret Act.

Considering this matter in relation to the killing of Lumumber, I could not help wondering if the slave trade really had ended? Had it not simply re-emerged with a different face, a different method of operation, even if with substantially reduced numbers of casualties? But then, is any man really free? Former U.S. President John F. Kennedy hit the nail on the head with the acute observation that "Freedom is indivisible, and when one man is enslaved, all are not free." Notwithstanding the official abolition of the slave trade and the death of colonialism, the black man was still technically being enslaved and, in the case of Britain, that was a contributory fact to the glaring decadence eating through the infrastructure even in the face of marked industrial growth.

Not being spiritually inclined however, many of the British might not be aware of this very real decadence, let alone think of it in terms of the law of reciprocal action, or the law of sowing and reaping. Paying the aggregate price of colonial adventures. Now the subjects of those former colonies, the off-springs of those former slaves, have thronged its shores, bringing all their discordant habits and cultural traits with which to merge with British refinement, forging a multi-ethnic discoloration of the hitherto unblemished purity of whiteness that finds it difficult to stand the test of compromise.

There have been clashes, there have been riots, there have been killings, permeated with a thread of perpetual tension that will never go away. While the men of colour have been emerging largely second-best in the messy confrontations, both sides have suffered an equal share of pain, despair, suspicion and uncertainty as to what tomorrow may bring, and for the native Briton, things can never be the same again.

The Empire has been cremated, there is no more butter for the superior British bread, the streets of London are no longer paved with gold, and black hornets whose jungle nests colonialism had the effrontery to tamper with, have become bent on sharing in the residue of their own estate, which was transferred to Britain. Full marks for Ed Howe's wisdom: "We are not free, it was not intended we should be. A book of rules is placed in our cradle, and we never get rid of it until we reach our graves. Then we are free, only then."

~

Free but not forgotten. Lumumber was finally accorded this blessed freedom, having put up a spirited fight to enforce his fundamental human rights. To place the reasons for his death in their proper prospective, I found the need to find out everything I could about the legendary Congolese freedom fighter, Patrice Lumumber, thinking there might just be some spiritual link to be drawn with his ill-fated namesake of Pentonville prison.

I found out that they had actually been brothers in the true sense of the word. Patrice Lumumber, Marxist ex-Prime Minister of The Congo, had been killed under mysterious circumstances on 17th January 1961, following a protracted showdown with his former Portuguese overlords. Moscow, in an angry reaction, charged the then-UN Secretary General, Dag Hammarskjold, with complicity. In retrospect, it seemed impossible to ignore the fact that the military regime of the then-Colonel Joseph Mobutu (later titled Field Marshal Mobutu Sese Seko) had directly overseen the murder of Patrice Lumumber.

It was the same regime of Mobutu,

destined to be in power for 32 years, doubtless stricken with fear, insecurity, and a guilty conscience, which hounded and harassed the brother of the murdered Congo Premier into seeking political sanctuary off-shore.

It reminds me of the kind of discussions I used to have with the only ethnic-minority governor at the 'Ville (Pentonville). He was of Asian origin and was quite proud of his achievements. We used to have one-on-one conversations about racism and the best ways of combating it.

"Michael, if you take it on the chin and accept any racial insults and slurs, it's not necessarily a bad thing; if only to enhance your chances of promotion."

I disagreed and pointed out so much, "No,

I don't think it helps – it's attitudes like that, which have helped entrench racial divisions."

"But, with further promotions, I will eventually get to a position where I will be able to make a real difference," he said with a convincing nod. I applauded this laudable ideal but pointed out that with the current structure of the service, his future position would be so isolated as to be actually ineffectual. Moreover, we happened to be holding this conversation in his office, which was discernibly different from the many other governors' offices in the 'Ville.

His office was the only one without any windows. Need I say more!

After this conversation, I was still hopeful,

if pessimistic, that racism in the system, as well as the system itself, could be changed from the inside out. Change happens. I could be the one to fill those big shoes to make changes, stamp out injustice, make a difference.

However, after Lumumber's death, I was sapped of my hope, and respect for the prison service, and even justice. Yet, as I began to change – instead of being able to change the system around me – I had no clue that I was heading toward another life-shaking encounter. It happened around about the time my fellow officers set upon me like a dog in the street. As the first knuckle pounded my cheek, and I fought for consciousness… It was a monumental turning/breaking point in my life.

But, Lumumber's death was really the match that lit the fuse. And from that moment on, right up until the mob-attack two years later, the tensions were building – inside me, and inside Pentonville. Inevitably, the breaking point was just around the corner.

Chapter Five

"Liberty is the only thing you can't have unless you give it to others."

~ *William Allen White*

Like the turning of the seasons, I sensed a change within myself. There were changes within the establishment, too. The authorities showed good sense by ordering that all the inmates be locked up after the killing of Lumumber. Without such a precautionary move, riots would most certainly have broken out among the black inmates. No matter how much I philosophized, no matter how much I hated what happened; nothing would reverse this tide that began when Lumumber's life ended.

The racial tension that blanketed Pentonville Prison for much of the next week was like some thick fog of expectation, tinged with uncertainty as to the source or the manner with which more bloody trouble would manifest itself. Two days of hunger strike and mass disobedience from the black inmates ensued when news of Lumumber's unlawful killing broke out, fired by vocal outrage and threats of murder. Security was beefed up inside the prison, and police were drafted in.

At the end of the day it came to nothing, but left a bitter taste that would remain for a long time. I, being one of just a handful of non-white prison officers, contributed in a major way to dousing the flames, with my usual flair for diplomacy.

Yet still, for me, inclination and duty became locked in stalemate. The helplessness of the incarcerated black prison inmates and the sadness and tragedy of being detained, under murky circumstances, together threw a shameful light on the penal system. This would not and should not excuse the injustice meted out by the offenders on their victims, but there had to be some effective median that could kill two birds with one stone? A way to make the prison service obsolete and, at the same time, inculcate the sense of responsibility that would remove the killer/destruction instinct in the potential offender?

The late Heinrich Heine's rather pearly proposal for a remedy may seem too philosophical in an era when it is no longer fashionable to think in terms of God:

If thy tongue offend thee, tear it out.
If thine eye offend thee, pluck it out.
If thy hand offend thee, cut it off
And if thy brain offend thee, turn Catholic.

But having started to identify more and more with the black inmates since Lumumber's slaying, and in consequence gaining their confidence, that was the one remedy I relied upon (in a casual way) to seduce them away from a life of crime and all the trappings of it.

Thus, I made myself as approachable as was reasonably possible - vis-à-vis acceptable officer-prisoner relationships. There was a tendency for many inmates to see me in leadership terms as their only source of hope, inspiration and sanity. The black man is a spiritual animal and therein lies his only true source of salvation in an oppressive racist system; one that's becoming more atheistic by the day. If I had been able to swap my authoritative prison officer's uniform for the more becoming cleric's robe, I am confident that I would have amassed a great following among the black inmates of Pentonville. Desiring to gain my favour and sympathy, they needed to ascertain what made me tick, and they came to understand that it was matters divine.

Not without tests though; as one would expect from such a closely confined environment as this barred sanctuary for convicts, the potential for violence was limitless. In my early days, I was lucky enough to recognise the adage: "You have nothing to fear but fear itself." I couldn't possibly remember the countless times an inmate threatened me with violence, but as I learned to embrace that fear, I found out that it turned mostly negative situations into positive.

~

“I’m going to break your jaw, you fucking screw!” the inmate snarled.

“Yeah, you see this junction between the jaw line, just make sure you break it properly. That way, when I get my compensation, I’ll be on a Caribbean beach, drinking to your health and you’ll have another X amount of years added to your sentence.”

It used to crack me up the way the expressions changed as realisation dawned. “You’re mad, crazy.”

"Now will you do as you are told?"

"All right, Guv!"

It gave me a refreshing insight into the mind of the criminal. When they take you into their almost impenetrable confidence to bare their entire soul to you, they present an impressionable audience for you to implant the roots of counseling. You see sensitive, vulnerable souls essentially made for a simple, happy way of life, basically good-natured, managing within the tight circle of their exposure to education to make the best of the little that is available in a fiercely competitive and discriminatory system.

Once, they cherished liberty - as does everyone else who understands that the God who gave us life, also gave us liberty at the same time. But, these prisoners had not been schooled in the fine art of channeling that liberty in such a successful way as to benefit themselves and society and to enable them to honour the God they ultimately worship.

It was now left solely at my door to try and impart to them the philosophy of Henry Brooks Adams as a living truth: "Absolute liberty is absence of restraint, responsibility is restraint therefore the ideally free individual is responsible to himself." But, there was a crucial flaw in that matter of responsibility...

I would say that George Bernard Shaw understood it very well. "Liberty means responsibility. That is why most men dread it."

Frank Cane was no less appreciative of its importance in the lives of men, yet was constrained to acknowledge that it is man's most daunting challenge in life. "Responsibility is the thing people dread most of all. Yet it is the one thing in the world that develops us, gives us manhood or womanhood fibre."

So, in my new quest to court the confidence and trust of inmates, I took pains to philosophize on the invaluable worth of self, the duty of every individual to justify, redeem and preserve that divine gift with conduct that respects the sanctity of his fellow human being, and in turn reciprocally attract high esteem and perhaps more from others around them. But, of course, I am but one man, and only human.

~

My whole attitude towards prison reforms differed significantly from both the British liberal and conservative approach, and it was with my candid outlook on the matter that I sought in earnest to impress the many black inmates who flocked over to me for protection and help. As I saw it, the way forward was in the recognition, on the part of the offender, of his responsibility and the gravity of his offence. The gentle but firm and earnest counseling would be calculated to open his eyes to the seriousness of the injury to his victim, its possible long-term effects, and his recognition that he was duty-bound to contribute to the healing of that injury one way or the other.

Once that first step of acquiescence in

principle, to his culpability was successfully taken, then community jobs would be created in which he would be obliged to participate. He would be paid commensurate remuneration for the job, his board and upkeep in prison being deducted from his pay. A large percentage of his moneys would be forfeited to his victim as a means of assuming responsibility for his crime, such forfeiting being accepted in good faith and with a sense of remorse. The balance of his remuneration would be given to him at the end of his sentence to enable his starting a new life. One free of crime and with a future less fearful of responsibility.

This was my remedy. Unfortunately, it fell on deaf ears during officers' meetings, and it never appeared to stand any chance of being taken to higher quarters within

Pentonville. The principle of an eye-for-an-eye appeared to appeal to the sadistic instincts of most prison officers, as basically rooted in both the liberal and conservative approaches to prison reforms. My approach was punitive enough, and costs would be excessive in terms of time, patience and endurance.

According to James Redford's "Celestine Insights", the liberals were of the view that people who had grown up in an abusive and oppressive situation were a product of their environments and would still yield to the influence of such environments in the absence of sound punitive corrective reprisals that could defy their negative influence. The conservatives on the other hand viewed the principle of stopping a life of crime and violence as being merely a matter of taking a conscientious choice.I ascertained that both views, vis-à-vis the current evolution of man, appear to have severe shortcomings. The liberal approach merely skims the surface - in the sense that liberals believe people can embrace change if offered different circumstances and better financial support or education. Moreover, intervention programmes - as a means of facilitating purification effects - focus only on helping others to better their decision making and economic choices. In the case of violent offenders, rehabilitation attempts have invariably offered superficial counseling at best; excuse and leniency at worst. This is a precise recipe for disaster, for every time the offender is slapped on the hand and turned loose without consequences, it amounts to an encouragement to the offender to continue in that line of iniquitous behaviour, as if indeed such conduct is relatively innocuous - or, at any rate, not that serious. At the end of the day, the perfect scenario is set for its inevitable re-occurrence. The circle of bad behaviour continues ever onwards.

Similarly, of course, the negativity of the alternative eye-for-an-eye conservative approach of an eye-plucking has this re-cycling boomerang effect on the society. It also has one thing in common with its liberal counterpart: both want to solve these social problems by following avenues that effectively relegate the offender, that is to say the offender is basically told of things to do in order to correct his behaviour. That remedy falls into the pigeonhole of 'irresponsibility'.

For as long as we fail to address the issue of responsibility, we will inadvertently fail to correct these social anomalies. These two approaches cannot be more succinctly put than in Henry Ford II's assertion: "You will find men who want to be carried on the shoulders of others, who think that the world owes them a living. They don't seem to see that we must all lift together and pull together."

~

I have to admit, however, that I did not start to hold strongly to my approach of lifting and pulling together; not until the killing of Lumumber. This occasion opened my hitherto bat's eye-view of the black problem with a keener hawk-eyed glare. I believe that throughout my life, I have essentially been a compassionate individual, with an abhorrence of injustice or hardship (even where self-imposed, as in the case of prison inmates). Prior to Lumumber's killing - and notwithstanding my generally cynical attitude towards the self-aggrandizement of white supremacists - I was sympathetic to white and black inmates alike; colour-blind, so to speak. I equally wanted both to be out of here as soon as possible, hopefully having learnt their lesson, and back in the mainstream of public life, to serve society and God. Was I naïve, foolish perhaps? Or living true to myself and my faith?

At that time, my attitude of the penal system more or less embraced the liberal approach, having personally lived and breathed the way of life that catered for all sorts of seamier sides of human nature. I could thus identify, I could empathise, I could understand. But if ever I was in any doubt that the black man's colour was being used as the basis of a policy to oppress him; the killing of Lumumber erased that doubt once and for all.

Henceforth my hitherto liberal approach to the penal system underwent a revision, nurtured principally with all inmates in mind. Admitting this to myself, I could not overlook that both the British liberal and conservative approaches were giving birth principally with white British inmates in mind.

Two parallel lines were at play here, there was my approach to the penal system, essentially with sympathies for all the inmates at Pentonville, including those who happened to be people of colour; and there was the approach of the all-conquering British policymakers, essentially catering for kith and kin.

Understandably, my outlook was threatened with a stillbirth, with the white colleagues who heard them well aware that by now I had become something of a champion in the eyes of the black inmates in Pentonville. So, I found myself in the very dilemma of the black people whose cause I had now committed myself to championing. I had invariably placed my neck alongside theirs on the proverbial chopping block. Yet, I was in the vast majority with virtually no voice of opinion that could be heard beyond the threshold of my own mind. This posture against the prevailing policies of a racist establishment was not destined to go very far, if anywhere at all.

Nevertheless, still satisfied that there was the need for black folk to organise on a policy to extricate the race from eternal damnation on earth, I carried out my duties for Her Majesty's Prison Service with this attitude toward the penal system, fraternising with black inmates to the limits that the rules of my calling permitted, being strong and firm where there was the need to be so, and bending over backwards when there was the need for that. I would give them the benefit of the doubt that the system never afforded them. Why? Because I could. Because it made a difference. Because if fate had played a different hand, I could have been in their shoes, perhaps – instead of patrolling the cells from the outside of the bars.

Inmates who attempted to take advantage of the receptiveness I had reserved exclusively for them, misinterpreting it as an expedient cover with which to project a falsified innocence, encountered my disapproval of criminality of any description, be it perpetrated either by black or white. They saw that I kept a strict regard for the truth and sought to live and breathe this policy to the penal system, as manifested by my regular counseling on the right attitudes to life and civilised conduct.

My metamorphosis was nearing completion, and this was the butterfly that emerged from the chrysalis of change. The prisoners saw the colour of my wings, and it was apparent they didn't match the other officers on duty. Furthermore, I believe that one of the factors that helped to punctuate my efforts to tame the black inmates with a measure of success was the Nelson Mandela story - the legend of a black hero who had risen to the pedestal of glory by virtue of having been an inmate in an oppressive white system. It tickled the fancy of virtually every black inmate it was my experience to liaise with, and it became branded like a permanent emblem of pride on the black mind.

The Nelson Mandela story had become like the Black Bible to every black inmate, and because it seemed to be a source of inspiration to me, my motivating factor, the Pentonville prisoners quickly adopted it as a driving force to get the hell out of prison. The black inmates felt proud to be able to identify with Mandela, but without losing touch with the reality of having committed a crime against society, which Mandela did not.

While it would have been a betrayal to the system on my part to sympathise with the generality of black inmates as to deceive them into believing themselves innocent of the charges against them, hence working against the interest of the establishment that had employed me, I satisfied my conscience that it was the racist policy of subjugation by the supremacists which created the circumstances that landed most blacks in prison. Hence my avowed commitment to prison reforms.

~

The reality was bleak. Three-quarters of the West Indian black population in Britain were scarcely educated, expressing themselves in barely literate sentences. Most had been excluded from primary school. No real incentive by the British government had been put in place to consider their special cultural circumstances and effectively encourage and promote the virtues of education. Their decline was facilitated by the easy availability of drugs to black youths, which would lead on to crime, and then on to prison, helping to fulfill and fuel immortal myths about inherent black inferiority.

While the West Indian black people in Britain amounted to a negligible two percent of the total British 60 million population, when calculated on a pro rata basis, there were more blacks in British prisons than their white counterparts.

As a black man, and prison officer, it was very difficult to accept this, especially recognising the existence of a very definite conspiracy to suppress the black race. By and large, I figured that these black inmates were victims of a subtle and complex scheme to allocate them to a zoological order; a situation clearly calculated to defy every kind of corrective measure that would make them eligible for prison reforms! So even with my approach to prison reforms for all, well-meaning and patriotic as they were, I sometimes felt as if I was running up an escalator that was going down as fast in the opposite direction. However, I was more clear than ever that only my approach would better the circumstances of black offenders; and even at that, there was no guarantee that the reformed black ex-inmate walking along the pavement, quietly minding his own business, would not be pounced upon by the police, to be unfairly brutalised and charged with loitering with intent and assaulting police officers.

Before the twinkling of an eye, he is back

in prison. Back where he "belongs."

This familiar tale of blatant racist victimisation assailed my years in Pentonville more times than I care to remember, to say nothing of the more numerous accounts heard in the open society over many years.

I was convinced that a significant number of black inmates in Pentonville had no reason for being there, and accordingly I could see why my counseling on the virtues of humility, peace and faith in God was being misapplied to inmates who knew themselves to be blameless and innocent of the charges that dumped them in jail.

Spiritually, I could sense that my growing popularity with the black inmates was not going down well with the prison authorities. By rights it should have done, because there was a marked reduction in rebelliousness from the black camp of Pentonville, and this became ongoing at the height of my approach to prison reforms. But, there's no pleasing some people...

~

One can well appreciate why the black inmates invariably proved to be the most problematic of all racial groups in British prisons. With the possible exception of the Jews, the plight of the black race was the most hopeless and pathetic of all. It was my ability to recognise this disquieting reality after the killing of Lumumber. It became possible for me, in my newly awakened state, to be propelled into action in a bid to contribute my little quota in redressing the situation. Doubtless my stance would attract the clichéd charge of having a chip balanced on my shoulder, but I feel vindicated from such a charge when I recall that the same view was echoed with colourful eloquence by no less a personality than President Abraham Lincoln of America in the 19th century, who was quoted thus: "When you have succeeded in dehumanising the Negro, when you have put him down and made it impossible for him to be but as the beasts of the field, when you have extinguished his soul in this world and placed him where the ray of hope is blown out as in the darkness of the damned, are you quite sure that the demon you have roused will not turn and rend you?"

On that last word, the brutal point has

been scored. All that remains is a final summing up showing that the racial situation of the modern era has not significantly changed since the Abraham Lincoln period, except that the supremacist policymakers have become cleverer in covering their tracks and refining their prejudices. The same frustrations and hopelessness are felt by the victims, at every turn in life. Likewise the attitude of the dominant race still echoes the more blatant venom spewed out by 19th century author and supremacist Charles Carrol:

"The Negro is a beast, but created with articulate speech, and hands, that he may be of service to his master - the white man."

With this scenario prevailing in practical

reality, it is little surprising that while only eight percent of London's population were of black ethnicity, a ridiculously high percentage - almost 60 percent - of those arrested in the city for robbery offences were black people. The demon was turning to rend them.

In the Nottingham area, while only about 1.5 percent of the population was black, almost 25 percent of those arrested for robbery were black. The demon was turning to rend them.

In the Manchester area, while almost 1.5 percent of the population was black, disproportionately almost 15 percent of those arrested for robbery were black. The demon was turning to rend them.

And even in faraway USA, whilst the

blacks represented a bare fifth of the total population, over three quarters of prisoners arraigned on murder charges were black. The demon was turning to rend them.

Here I was, without regret or remorse. I was in uniform, yet identifying with opponents of the system. I was satisfied that I was performing an essential social service, more than that, perhaps, I was serving Truth, I hoped. And moreover God was the living Truth.

I no longer cared if I was not being discreet enough in the way I fraternised with the black inmates, and that quietly my superiors were frowning down on it. My fraternisation was yielding positive results. I was bringing the black inmates to heel. I was making the job of my white superiors easier. I was helping reform so many black inmates, and helping to make the streets a safer place. If my approach towards prison reforms was not being appreciated, it had to be because I was denying my superiors their sadistic satisfaction of feeding on the growing frustration of blackness? The number of helpless bear chains for the wild dogs to bait and hack to pieces was diminishing in the wake of my attitude.

I was spoiling their pastime of 'nigger-baiting,' 'nigger-bashing,' by imparting humility among black inmates. Too many black inmates were getting out for good behaviour, hence supposedly taking the spice out of prison work.

Of course I could not rule out, and did not rule out, the matter of envy. I suppose there is nothing quite like the glory of being placed in favourable limelight, when one is being uplifted in the image of a hero for one exemplary deed or other. And, in such a situation, there was bound to be envy to contend with.

Mixed with that envy, I was sure, was my evident refusal not to be a bootlicker, an Uncle Tom, not to be used to camouflage and perpetuate the ingrained policy of subjugation against my own.

"Of service to his master - the white man"? Not really. More a case of the thief who would not be set to catch his fellow thief.

I cannot actually recall any occasion of open encouragement or congratulatory gesture from my superiors, and I was in no doubt they were not in a hurry to entertain my own occasional fantasy about promotion. Certainly, here was one rare case where great minds could not think alike.

~

Entering into 1993, my reputation for reforming hardened inmates continued to grow, together with the popularity amongst these certain segments of the prison population. Virtually every other crisis involving recalcitrant black inmates, which threatened to get out of hand, saw me being summoned from wherever I was to intercede and save the day. Even among my white superiors, I had been tacitly promoted to an exalted status that recognised me as a factor for peace among the black inmates, who in turn appeared to regard me as their mouthpiece on every issue pertaining to their welfare and their fate. I was a go-between, stuck in the middle, too black to be 100% officer, too officer to be 100% the black inmates' brother-at-arms.

One particular memorable event in this ego-boosting involved a black inmate with a head as tall as the sky, a physique which would have made Charles Atlas blush with envy, and a scowl which would have frozen Mike Tyson in his tracks. He had just received a Life Sentence at the Old Bailey and had been brought back to the Ville to be processed. After a verbal altercation with a white officer, he reacted like a gorilla with murder in mind. One massive hand was clasped around the neck of the hapless officer, who was burly by normal standards, and the prisoner appeared ready to eat the officer alive if things degenerated against his wishes. I doubt if any amount of martial arts expertise could have extricated even a grandmaster from such a formidable opponent, and even with all his training in that respect the officer was not foolish enough to attempt any Bruce Lee suicide maneuvers.

On cue, I was summoned from the staff room, passing some anxious black inmates who declared, "They're trying to lynch another brother." Arriving on the scene, I encountered a tense and chilling scenario where about a dozen beefy battle-ready officers were being held at bay, shields and truncheons poised, by the enraged black inmate threatening to throttle the life out of the frozen officer.

Echoing off the walls, he bellowed, "If any of you mother-fuckers even dare to breathe near my ass..."

It was a delicate situation, to say the least, which had to be handled with the utmost tact if tragedy were to be averted. I waded in cautiously. He was well known to me, that West Indian powerhouse. If he had utilised his fists in the ring with the same savage invincibility as he had displayed in mugging activities, he would have been rubbing financial shoulders with the likes of Mohammed Ali and Larry Holmes, instead of undergoing corrective punishment behind bars. Delicately, I inched my way up to him and made the humble plea. "Look, why not hold my neck instead?"

This only served to provoke a series of deranged obscenities against his shaking white prey. I was in no doubt he was ready to die fighting, but making sure he took his captive with him to the grave. I tried Oscar Wilde's philosophy: "Always forgive your enemies, nothing annoys them so much."

This behemoth began frothing and screaming; his eyes swirling pools of black madness. I tried pleading the logic of William Shenstone: "Think, when you are enraged at anyone, what would probably become of your sentiments should he die during the dispute."

As he succumbed to silence but continued to breathe fire, I tried the Gerald W. Johnson approach – "No man was ever endowed with a right without being at the same time saddled with a responsibility."

Realisation appeared to dawn in his now cooling eyes. I drew his attention to my own plight as a strategy for the final finishing touch - courtesy Rainer Maria Erilke. "Do not believe that he who seeks to comfort you lives untroubled among the simple and quiet words that sometimes do you good. His life has much difficulty and sadness and remains far behind yours. Were it otherwise he would never have been able to find those words." Whereupon the giant released the neck of his lowly adversary, dropped his head on my shoulder and wept like a baby!

Three cheers for this acute observation by Dr. Robert Anthony: "The angry people are those people who are most afraid."

~

That year, 1993, was probably the most discouraging that one could recall in the monumental struggle to reform the free sinful world, let alone prison inmates.

In January, for instance, the Sicilian Mafia boss Salvatore Riina was arrested after eluding capture for 22 years.

In that year, British Prime Minister John Major rejected the idea of pardon for World War One servicemen executed for cowardice or desertion on the grounds that it would be "rewriting history."

Car bombs in Bombay, India, killed 200 people.

President de Klerk admitted that South Africa possessed nuclear weapons.

Chris Hani, the black South African Communist leader who might have succeeded Nelson Mandela as the voice of negritude in South Africa, was assassinated.

Two white Los Angeles policemen were found guilty of brutalising black American Rodney King.

One billion pounds worth of damages was caused by an IRA bomb which exploded in the city of London.

A siege in Waco, Texas, by a cult group ended with a fire that killed 97 people, among them their charismatic leader David Koresh.

Tennis champion Monica Seles was stabbed by a dissatisfied spectator during a match in Hamburg.

The President of Sri Lanka, Ranasinghe Premadasa, was assassinated by a suicide bomber.

The chairman of Polly Peck, Asil Nadir, jumped bail and ran away to Cyprus.

United Nations troops of Pakistani origin in Somalia shot into a crowd killing 20 people.

Islamic fundamentalists protesting against Salman Rushdie's book Satanic Verses carried out an arson attack on a hotel in Turkey killing 40 people.

Two eleven year old boys in Liverpool, England were convicted of murdering two year old James Bulger.

Boris Yeltsin, President of Russia,

declared a state of emergency after the worst outbreak of political violence since the Russian revolution in 1917.

These incidents share in common that they made a mockery of the essence of law enforcement, and made an even greater joke of the calling of prison officers in the glaring demonstration that people outside the walls of the penal system are free and that is why they are lost...

However much one knocks Britain's penal system, prison work represents one of the most daunting challenges in interaction with men. Even police work or military life appears to offer greater camouflage and protection by comparison. The soldier or policeman has tremendous room or space for maneuver, he has a wide expanse of land stretching out to the horizon to separate him from a potential adversary, affording him all the time to plan, hide and take evasive action. Not so the prison officer, who is literally confined within a limited space, behind locked doors, often with a group of highly dangerous men of questionable mental stability.

In his calling, the prison officer - every day - is walking a tightrope, his senses taut and alert, his nerves at full stretch. If one imagines the King Cobra locked in a room with half a dozen volatile mongooses, which he hopes have been tamed sufficiently to respect his authority and not turn wild, I think one has a pretty clear picture of the dicey nature of the prison officer's calling.

The raucous punch-ups between inmates will not leave him unscathed after he has helped in restoring calm. He has had jaws dislocated, lips remodeled, eyes blackened and teeth loosened at the hands of deranged and powerful men, and on sundry instances of monumental struggles on the floor, he has come close to losing his manhood. The prison experience sees excesses of the diabolical in the human make-up.

So it made perfect sense, and was right and fitting, that the pay for prison officers should be generous for such a high-risk undertaking, his other benefits no less attractive. My home, in a choice district of North London, was an enviable semi-detached structure with the appearance of a semi-luxurious modern villa. Rented by Her Majesty's Prisons, it had an almighty back garden, which provided the ideal venue for many a barbecue and other social get-togethers. And for the prison officer who needed nothing less than such a compensating tonic for working in hell, in the final analysis of good and evil, the challenge of his work; everything more or less evened out.

By and large, I was deriving job satisfaction in Pentonville; euphoria and a sense of accomplishment at home. Maybe these adjectives could have been different if my features bore the cuts and bruises of my less fortunate colleagues. But, it is a striking fact that in all the physical struggles to restrain and subdue combative inmates, every hair of mine remained in place. I felt this could be explained by the respect and leadership which I was fortunate to enjoy from most inmates, and I was determined to ensure that there was no change in this most favourable situation.

Alas however, I was destined to become a typical victim in a situation - enshrouded in an observation that I had read somewhere - one fleeting moment of joy can usher in months of misery.

While there was a real sense of satisfaction to be felt over the hard reality that the black inmate was not incorrigible as supremacist theories would have the world believe, there was a corresponding sense of dismay and hopelessness over the painful truism that the policy makers of the British system were bent on enforcing that notion on a permanent basis, as though it were a sacred truth.

This brought on a sense of despondency when it seemed that the encouraging headway I had made in reforming black inmates was essentially a waste of time in the face of a prevailing policy to keep them suppressed, using all the machinations available to achieve this. Could one man fight the system and expect realistically to win? The alternative was to organise a civil war in Britain, allowing the blacks the freedom to breathe real fresh air. I actually found myself soaring to that height of fantasy and wishful thinking.

Be that as it may, I believe that if I had been less spiritual than I was (or not spiritual at all) at the same time over-complacent and too self-satisfied over my successes in the quest to reform black inmates, I might have been unaware of the resentment quietly building up among my superiors in my direction. The tide was turning against me and my ways.

I began to tune in fully to this reality circa mid-1994. It was like a gradual spreading of a net of conspiracy, as if it were felt by others that I was getting 'too big for my boots.' I did not care that much, if at all believing that in the absence of having flouted any rules, or working against the interests of Her Majesty's government, there was little my superior officers could do by way of victimisation.

In retrospect I believe now, and suspected at the time, that what might have really touched a nerve was my fearless display of the new powers that had been accorded me. Not that I had been promoted as such, but maybe it could be seen as an upgrading of my status in recognition of my commitment and result-oriented approach to prison reform.
But, I have since come to wonder whether

it was some subtle test to ascertain how far I would dare to go in upsetting the apple cart. I had been conferred powers somewhat in the realm of allocation officer, though not strictly in that capacity, and it was now within my authority to investigate the circumstances of certain categories of inmates and make the appropriate recommendation or queries. Now, like in all civil service departments where it was the practice to break the rules within the safety and protection of the Official Secrets Act, the rights of men were often trampled on with impunity. It was especially easy to do so with victims who were cowed by the system and did not know such rights even existed.

In the penal system, there were some inmates who should not strictly have been behind bars in the first place, not having been officially remanded by a court of competent jurisdiction; others were not released when they had served their terms; some were in protective custody (for want of a reason for detaining them); otherwise there were inmates who were being held at the discretion of the prison authorities, based on a conviction that their continuing detention was in the best interests of all concerned, but without the legal backing to enforce such decisions.

As it turned out, almost all such victims were black inmates, and in most cases they had been beneficiaries of my approach to reformation. That is to say, while I was of the fervent opinion that their release from detention was well-deserved, the authorities of Pentonville Prison did not share that view and felt the need to prolong their stay.

Ultimately, when the hapless victims came complaining to me, as happened on at least a number of occasions, I in turn queried the appropriate department with a terse phone call, and in most cases after adequate investigations a release would be effected forthwith.

This served to upset the apple cart; one apple at a time, they came tumbling out. Once it was on record that such an order had been given by an authorising officer (I always followed it up in writing) and such release was legally due, it became extremely dangerous to disregard it. Nobody wanted to be held responsible. On sundry occasions, these developments brought me into quite heated exchanges with my superiors. Invariably I stuck to my guns, and invariably the release was effected. Each time, though, it was like a black mark was placed against my good name. They were keeping count and they were not pleased.

Yet, I was often grateful for the rebellious feature of my make-up, which served to embolden me in situations - especially if a cause was involved in which I conscientiously believed - where I would otherwise have backed down. I had read Clarence Darrow, and had been suitably impressed, grimly inspired by his statement: "As long as the world shall last, there will be wrongs, and if no man objected and no man rebelled, those wrongs would last forever." But, Lawrence Durrell was quick to point out an opposing view, "No one can go on being a rebel too long without turning into an autocrat."

I could not by any stretch of the

imagination be regarded as an autocrat, and for sure I had no ambitions in that direction. But, just as surely; my superiors regarded me as an insufferable pain, an embarrassing thorn in the hide of the Prison establishment. I was aware that anyone telling the truth in life has to have one foot in the stirrup. I was always careful to ensure that my tone to my superiors was couched with the requisite deference, which would nullify any charge of insubordination. Though I was unflinching in my contention that I had a keener insight than they did into the psychology of the black inmates over whom I held sway and thus was better placed to help in their rehabilitation.

Regardless, my superiors were obviously needled. It was a delicate situation, because any official action against me risked repercussions that might not be palatable to the establishment in these race-conscious days. Yet, spiritually I was aware that all they required was a cogent reason such as any wrong step I took, or any flouting of any rule, that would enable them to take justifiable punitive action. I provided them with none. I could sense that I had become persona non grata.

~

In the closing months of 1994 the tension between them and me could be sliced out of thin air with a knife. I effected the release of two more inmates during that period. The authorities had nothing further to say. As Calvi Coolidge rightly observed, "If you don't say anything, you won't be called to repeat it." But Charles De Gaulle had once warned that "Silence is the ultimate weapon of war." And that was my major concern where my superiors were concerned.

I anticipated the brewing of war clouds of sorts, and I rather suspected that I would not emerge victorious at the end of the day.

How right I was. The vicious attack on my person by my colleagues in the early hours of 17th December 1994 marked the beginning of the war calculated to remove me, permanently, from the British Penal System.

Chapter Six

"The man who fears suffering is already suffering from fears"

~ Michel de Montaigne

"The greatest mistake you can make in life is to continually be afraid you'll make one"

~ Elbert Hubbard

Fear can be a terrible emotion. Worse is the corroding psychological effect of uncertainty rooted in anticipation of horrendous, unmanageable consequences. In the words of Robert Antony, "The thing we run from is the thing we run to."

The policeman who had blackmailed me into withdrawing my charges against my assailants had effectively planted (no doubt deliberately) the seed of fear that I faced some terrible immeasurable harm if I pursued my claims. Still reeling as I was from the shock of what happened to Lumumber, I was satisfied that I could be confronting forces ruthless enough to dispense upon me the same rough justice. That fear haunted me even in my decision to pursue redress outside the long arm of police law enforcement, and it deepened in intensity with every lost minute of sleep.

Even my medical examination report from Islington Police Station was distorted and indecipherable, as you can see below.

ANNEXE C

METROPOLITAN POLICE

Medical Examination and Fees 534808

This form is not a Statement

Serial No.
Stn. Code:
Cus. No.:
TO 11:
Other ref.:

Part 1—to be completed by Doctor Tick boxes and delete as appropriate

Person examined/observed; Surname: Nsonwu Forenames: M

Place of examination/observation: Islington

Doctor's name: (BLOCK LETTERS) [illegible]

Examination/observation:

	Time	Date
began at	[illegible] am/pm	[illegible]
*ended at	[illegible] am/pm	

(inc. time taken to complete forms)

comprehensive clinical examination (RTA) ☐ blood sample: taken ☐

observation only ☐ other body sample(s): taken ☐

examination ☐ separate body chart completed

statement submitted ☐

Results of examination/observation

	YES	NO
Person examined/observed fit to be detained	☐	☐
Person examined/observed fit to be interviewed	☐	☐
Person examined/observed fit to be transferred	☑	☐
Police officer fit to continue duty	☐	☐

Claim for fees This is examination No.: 1 in on...

Claim in accordance with sub. para. ... of the scale of fees in the current PSSO Circ...

Claim for ......4..... miles travelled.

Total

GENERAL COMMENTS: (to include further details of treatment given, results, reasons for removal to hospital, treatment to be given in custody.)

[illegible handwritten comments]

Complete this section if examination/observation is in relation to an offence under S.4 Road Tra... 1988

	YES	NO
Evidence was found of disease or injury that might account for abnormal behaviour	☐	☐
In my opinion during the period of the examination/observation the ability of the person examined to drive a motor vehicle properly was impaired through alcohol ☐ drugs ☐	☐	☐
Evidence was found of alcohol ☐ drugs ☐ having been recently taken but during the period of the examination/observation of the person there was insufficient evidence to certify impairment.	☐	☐

Date: 17.12.99 Signature [signature]

If not a forensic medical examiner show full address

Part 2—to be completed by police

The Doctor:	Time	Date
arrived at	0050 am	17.12.99
left at	0130 am	17.12.99

Custody Officer:

I certify that the information in Part 2 is correct.

Signature [signature] 237

Name: PC [illegible] Rank/Divn No

BLOCK LETTERS

To add insult to injury, when the internal investigations started I realised, with dismay, that I - the aggrieved party and the accuser - was suddenly in danger of being painted as the villain.

The first shock came in a letter from a governor, J M Mason, concerning further use of the staff club: "I am instructed by Mr Abbott, governor, to inform you that your membership of the staff club has been suspended. This suspension will remain in force until the investigation into the incident has been completed." The others involved in the assault were similarly suspended, but that did not dim my outrage.

Next came notice of a disciplinary investigation, "to consider whether formal disciplinary proceedings should be initiated." It required no stretch of the imagination to deduce in a three-against-one situation, it was likely that I would be the one to attract disciplinary proceedings. It was clear the investigating panel felt obliged to adopt a middle-of-the-road impartiality on the strength of the misleading police reports that were created about the events of that night.

The police sergeant claimed: "Whilst this matter was being investigated, Mr Peter T attended the police station and made an allegation of assault against Mr Nsonwu. This allegedly occurred during the same incident, both Mr Nsonwu and Mr T subsequently decided to withdraw their allegations of assault, and witness statements were taken to that effect. There being insufficient evidence to substantiate any charge against

Mr David G; I released him from police detention at 4.20 a.m."

So, because of the ambiguity of the facts in evidence, from the outset the odds were stacked heavily in favour of my attackers. This remained very much the pattern during the investigative interviews. I have heard it said that income tax returns are the most imaginative fiction being written today, but I beg to differ. Even the combined literary efforts of Shakespeare, Dickens, and Shaw would have paled into significance against the creativity of the yarns that my attackers and their 'perjured' witnesses weaved.

In the intervening period, ill health got the better of me. Following a psychological evaluation at a mental clinic in February 1995, the clinical psychologist declared acute stress and psychological trauma, resulting in my enforced absence from work. I was losing everything, and it seemed inevitable that my mind would follow suit eventually.

Meanwhile, while I should have been resting and taking it easy, I wrote an angry letter to the Governor of Pentonville demanding that my attackers be suspended, pending enquiries, and asking for assurances that should my doctor declare me fit to return to work, I was not likely to experience another assault at their hands.

The response of the new Governor, Mr K Brewer, was basically evasive. "I'm not aware that you are in any danger from other members of staff, you are incorrect in believing that when allegations of assault are made, those involved should necessarily be suspended."

Why, I wondered, would the police have immediately arrested David on the strength of my allegations and visual evidence of bodily harm if that was untrue?

Furthermore, the findings did not appear to apportion any blame. The Investigating Governor, Mr Mason, said that it had been a difficult investigation because the incident occurred at the administration staff party and that recollections of many people there were hazy, due to alcohol, so it was difficult to make recommendations or formulate any charges against individual officers. He could offer two possibilities: A) that four of us be charged under the Prison Service Code of

Discipline for misconduct, i.e actions whether on or off duty bringing discredit on the Prison Service; B) the other option being to severely caution me and the two others and ban us from using the club for a fixed period. This should be a verbal warning backed up by a written one, which should be placed on each officer's record of service. Apparently I would be tarred with the same brush as those who beat me to a pulp!

Mr Mason didn't apparently take into account that it was I who had instigated this complaint, firstly by reporting it to the police, and then electing (for the sake of the prison service) to have the matter dealt with by the prison's internal disciplinary procedure. Considering that Mr Mason had been present some several hours after the incident when I reported it to the

Governor, and had seen my injuries when they were still fresh, the decision he arrived at following the preliminary investigation was, to say the least, perverse.

On his recommendation, a hearing took place to answer the charges of 'fighting.' It was an independent hearing, during which I questioned Mr Mason on the way he had conducted the investigation. It became abundantly clear to all and sundry that the charges of 'fighting' were wholly inappropriate. We were all acquitted of this charge.

What did emerge in evidence, however, was that I had been assaulted, and that Mr Mason had chosen an inappropriate charge in order to deny me a remedy. He must have been aware that, without this remedy, my career as a prison officer was at an end. He had given the clearest possible signal that the perpetrators of the racial assault could act with impunity, and I couldn't do a damn thing about it.

Certainly, imaginations did not have to be stretched to comprehend that Mr Mason was merely out to appease in a damage limitation exercise that would protect the image of the service.

Well, I did not mince words in my protest to Mr J Thomas Ferrand, the Group Equal Opportunities Officer. In fact, I pointed out that, when the police had told David that "It is alleged that you head-butted this man," David had replied: "He's been chatting up my girlfriend all night." Then he was promptly arrested for 'assault occasioning actual bodily harm.' By inference, as anyone with half a brain can deduce, David had admitted this offence. Meanwhile, his accusation of my 'chatting up his girlfriend' was not even part of his written evidence? Plus, the fact that I did not speak to, or touch, this mysterious girlfriend at any time that day or night, makes his utterance a lame defence.

I further pointed out in my protest that corroborative statements by my colleagues suggest I was in the lobby to use the payphone or to use the toilet facilities at the next bar. Yet, I had a mobile phone in my pocket, with free local calls from 1900hrs to 0700hrs. Why would I be in a darkened lobby using a pay phone? It was conceivable that I could have been on my way back from the toilet, but notes from Mr Mason's investigation show that I was seen urinating against the club wall shortly after the incident. This debunks the toilet theory and lends credence to my evidence that I was led to my doom in that corridor.

Nevertheless, the investigator failed to address these fundamental points that I have mentioned, leaving me no choice but to question the validity of this entire investigation. The fact of the matter is that this attack was the latest attempt in a culmination of ill-will and animosity, which so far I had been able to contain and channel. Then, this occasion afforded an opportunity for a physical attack.

In light of the foregoing, I felt obliged to take the matter to the Commission for Racial Equality. It became a big issue. The efforts of the Mason investigation to make a molehill out of a mountain were finally failing, and everybody started scrambling about to escape being roped into the very plagued subject of racial prejudice.

The gushing charm and anxiety reflected in John Thomas Ferrand's reply to my protest bore testimony to this truth. "Since you have written to me, in my capacity as head of Equal Opportunities for the Prison Service, I assume that you are lodging a grievance of alleged racial harassment. If this is the case, please will you provide written details of any other incidents, giving dates, times and names of those involved? In the meantime, I have spoken to your Governor, Mr K Brewer, who is familiar with your circumstances. I understand that you have been on sick leave since this incident occurred and that he has written to you earlier this year, urging you to return to work. I am sure that this will help you and your family in coming to terms with the aftermath of this unpleasant incident. I will write you again once I have discussed your case with Conduct and Performance Section, but please do not let this delay your return to work."

Although, the diplomatic delaying tactics, which could be discerned from this letter, was confirmed in his correspondence to the Conduct and Performance Section, which was more like a cry for help. "I have sent Mr Nsonwu a holding reply, pending advice from you on the conduct and performance issues.

"Since he has written to me, in my capacity as Head of Equal Opportunities and alluded to racial harassment, I have asked him to provide specific details. I should be grateful for your advice on how best to reply to Mr Nsonwu."

A response to that letter from the Equal Opportunities Manager merely stated: "If I can make any useful contribution to considering Mr Nsonwu's latest complaint (about the failure of managers at Pentonville adequately to investigate or act upon his earlier complaint of a racially motivated assault) please let me know." He might as well have added, "All yours, mate. Ta-ta for now!" or "Don't call us, we'll call you."

In August of 1995, a detailed medical report from the Brownlow Medical Centre to the Civil Service Medical Adviser, HM Prison Service, left no one in doubt that this wasn't just a small problem that could be ceremoniously swept beneath the carpet.

"I feel that Mr Nsonwu is unlikely to return to work until such time the case is resolved to his satisfaction. Mr Nsonwu does not suffer from any physical disability and the only disability that he could suffer in the future is the psychological disability trauma resulting from the assault, which he feels is racially motivated. This psychological disability is unlikely to continue for long provided he does not return to work in the same environment."

By this point, I had decided to take proceedings through a Race Relations Tribunal to indict Governor Mason and other prison staff for victimisation. I relayed this decision to the Principal Officer of the Personnel Department when he visited me at home without warning.

His mission was, essentially, to persuade me to return to work (I had been on half-pay since July), taking pains to remind me that a further 24-years lay ahead before retirement and that I should consider the remuneration and security for my family which prison service pay provides. He offered me a transfer to Wormwood Scrubs Prison so as to be in a different environment.

I told him that succeeding in my action through the Race Relations Tribunal was more important to me than money, and only after the outcome of the Tribunal's verdict could I consider whether and where to return to work.

The Principal Officer's subsequent report to the Governor of Pentonville Prison galled me, to say the least. There was absolutely no justification for the misleading impression conveyed. Hear him: "The conclusions I drew were that he has no intention of returning to work although there is nothing wrong with him, and thinks that he will obtain compensation through the Race Relations Tribunal so substantial that he will more than cover all loss of salary. Despite ninety minutes spent emphasising where his best interests lie, I could see that Mr Nsonwu is only interested in pursuing a campaign of retribution based on the delusion that there is a racially-orientated cause which he must champion."

I kid you not, my senior officer, who should supposedly have been subjective actually used the word *delusional* in his official report to his superiors without supporting medical evidence. God help me !

Throughout my discussions with this principal officer, I was aware of his anxiety that I should return to work. But, I was also satisfied that this anxiety was rooted in the prospect of any public taint on the image of Pentonville Prison as a "racist" institution, and represented a subtle effort to dissuade me from the course of going public with a charge of racism.

Though, for the first time in a long while, I wasn't losing any sleep over anxieties, especially any anxieties that **they** were harbouring. I simply waited for my moment.

~

The Race Relations Tribunal was held over three days, from 19 and 21 February 1996. The proceedings were registered as being brought against Governor Mason alone. But when it was pointed out that I had wanted to enjoin him together with his employers, Her Majesty's Prison Service, the Tribunal Chairman directed that the Secretary of State for the Home Department should be added as a Respondent. Moreover, the title of the proceedings was promptly amended to present the Secretary of State as the First Respondent and Mr Mason as the Second Respondent. My contention, for purposes of clarity, was that Mr Mason had discriminated against me on racial grounds by choosing charges that were inappropriate and which would leave me without an effective remedy.

As portrayed in the official record from the Industrial Tribunal, my motives were straightforward and pure:

"The Applicant is aged 35 and is black. Although born in the United Kingdom, the Applicant was brought up in Nigeria by his father, who was a police officer. The Applicant returned to this country in 1986 and, after a number of jobs, applied in 1990 to join the Prison Service. The Applicant said in his evidence, and we accept, that his motive for seeking employment as a Prison Officer was to help others."

But, at the end of the day, everything would hinge on the burden of proof. That had become quite clear when the Group Equal Opportunities Officer had asked me to provide specific details of incidents, dates, times and names of those involved in the alleged harassment. So even before the Tribunal started sitting, I was aware that the burden of proof, with its numerous shades of meaning and interpretations, would present something of a stumbling block, but not an insurmountable one if the truth were on my side. I knew that Mr Mason was a top-ranking Brother of the Masonic Fraternity - but still I was not daunted.

In the intervening period between the investigations and the sitting of the Race Relations Tribunal, I sought to push my case to the furthest levels in the corridors of power. I notified my local Member of Parliament, The Rt Hon Michael Portillo, and furnished him with all the facts. He in turn brought the matter to the notice of the then-Home Secretary, Michael Howard, who carried out his own enquiries before replying. The sum total of his findings was that if I could provide hard evidence of racial discriminations or harassment, appropriate steps would be taken to deal with the matter. While his reply was reassuring and written with the utmost good faith, I was prompted to open the eyes of my MP to a few other glaring facts which were overlooked by the Home Secretary.....

"Neither is the whole truth to say that the police decided to take no action. It was at the police station that another of my assailants alleged that I had assaulted him, and he indicated an injury to his thumb. To persuade me not to press charges, I was told that I would be locked up for the night at the station if I wished to proceed with the charges."

I and many other black people have a well-grounded fear of custody, for example I was talking to Lumumber's relative only a matter of minutes before he met his death in custody at Pentonville. While it is accurate to say that the Governor of Wormwood Scrubs concluded that the charges of 'fighting' could not be sustained, it was clear from the evidence that, had the charges of assault been brought against my assailants, such a charge would have stood an excellent prospect of success. This would be apparent from the tape recording of the Hearing. The decision to proceed with the unsafe and unsound charges of 'fighting' was made by Mr Mason. In the circumstances, the question of new evidence was not relevant. The appropriate course of action was for the proper charges to be brought against my assailants. In the meantime, my circumstances are that - since 21 October 1995 - I have been receiving no salary, when I ought to be suspended pending a resolution of this issue.

The major issue now was: what was the motive which one could lay against Governor Mason to link him with a charge of racial harassment? This went back to my formative months in the prison service.

~

I was completing my probationary year with the respondents, circa October 1991. At that time, Mr Mason held the rank of Principal Officer, and had become my line manager. He carried out a performance appraisal of my one-year probationary period; the procedure for determining whether an appointment should then be confirmed. He recommended that my one-year's probationary period be extended by a further three months. The reasons he gave were - my sickness record and my inability to get on with others. I was shocked and outraged.

To start with, the recommendation was irregular and discriminatory. The procedure that was supposed to be followed, and had been hitherto for my white colleagues, was that the contents of Mr Mason's report should be discussed with the probationer prior to the meeting before the Governor's Board. This afforded the probationer the opportunity to discuss the report and/or to prepare him for further discussions on the matter with the Board, chaired by Governor Kellis.

Seeing my emotional state, the Governor asked Mr Mason to leave the room. She then told me that I had the right of appeal, leaving me in no doubt that she could see the injustice of Mason's report. As if thinking aloud, she said, "These morons will try to bring you down." She then went on to say that she herself experienced sex discrimination in the past, not dissimilar to that which I was now encountering. She even explained that the correct procedure was that the report should have been shown to me before the Governor's Board Meeting.

When Mason returned to the room, Ms Kellis reprimanded him. Neither of the two criticisms contained in his report had any basis in fact. My sickness record was between 6 to 8 days of absence in the whole year, a far better record than most of my white peers. With regard to my alleged inability to get on with others, I had been involved in a couple of altercations with colleagues who displayed a marked absence of racial tolerance. But the incidents were storms in a teacup, never really becoming an issue. For sure the criticism was a contradiction to the testimonials I had received from earlier assessment ratings.

Finally, an aspect of the Mason report which particularly irked me was the fact that he had never brought up such matters as absences or personality problems. Since this was my probationary year, one would have supposed that its very nature demanded close monitoring, so that if any problem, correction, or adjustment was required, then it would have been raised as and when the need arose. Mr Mason, as my supervisor, at no time passed a single comment about my performance or my relationship with others.

Regardless, my appeal to the Home Office against the Mason report was successful. But, my extended three-month probationary period came and went before I heard anything from them. And it was only by chance that I found out they had written to me nearly four months before, in July. One day I called in at the Training Office to seek information on Open University courses. The person in charge was on the phone; as I waited, my gaze rested on an envelope pinned on the wall. The letter was addressed to me. "Oh, you weren't supposed to see that," he said.

I contended that since it was a letter addressed to me, I was entitled to take it and open it. The man panicked and phoned Governor Kellis. There and then Ms Kellis phoned the Home Office, who ordered that the letter should be given to me. I spoke to the Governor on the phone, and she explained that Mr Mason and other officers had been lobbying the Home Office to change their decision to cancel the extension of my probationary period.

After that, my life became unbearable. It was scandalous to think that a letter from the Home Office informing me of their decision had been deliberately withheld, so that I still went through the rigours of the additional three month probationary period successfully appealed against!

I was informed by a group of sympathetic colleagues that Mr Mason had accused me of being “big headed” and in relation to my appeal, had remarked, “I don’t know how the black bastard did that!”

Knowing the man’s nature and following

the warning from the Governor, I was satisfied that this was an accurate reflection of Mr Mason's attitude.

Ultimately, I was sent to Coventry by my colleagues (influenced as they were by Mason's anger) for having the audacity to challenge Mason, notwithstanding the success of that challenge.

Still, I was resolved to press on with my career and make the best of what was available. Then another shock came: suddenly and without any explanation, I was transferred out of my cherished OCA (Observation, Classification and Admissions). I felt I had made excellent progress in that category of prison work; it was interesting and called for good judgement, good sense and a sound intelligent capacity. As I mentioned, Mr

Mason was my line manager at the time, yet it was not he who told me I was being transferred. I had been there nine months, and was deriving tremendous job satisfaction from its challenging nature. To this day, I have no idea why I was transferred, so I can only suspect racial victimisation, once again.

I was moved to Externals - and work that was eminently uninteresting and lacked any meaningful challenge. Basically I accompanied prisoners to and from Court.

So, I carried out those duties for 15 months, during which I was confronted by another turn of events: my ASR (Annual Staff Reports) became progressively worse. For instance, I was given a 'Box 4' for report writing when I never once wrote a single report throughout that time!

In June 1994, I was transferred to duties in 'C' wing, and was permitted just six months therein before the final plan to remove me from the Prison Service manifested itself in the infamous beating-up.

~

As far as I was concerned, these facts and the discriminatory manner in which Mason conducted the investigations into the assault on me were sufficient to infer that he discriminated against me unlawfully. Since that time I had been unable to return to work, because of the psychological effects of Mr Mason's discrimination.

Of course, the final judgement was rendered by the Tribunal, delivered in the very familiar British strategy of anaesthetising a patient from the pain of the terrible blow about to be brought down upon him. Oh, the compassion that the Tribunal chairman expressed for poor Michael Nsonwu. Hear him!

"If the Applicant is correct in his account of the events, which took place on 17 December 1994, as to which we express no view, he must indeed have a considerable sense of grievance. The way in which matters fell out have resulted in no finding being made against any of the individuals concerned. The Applicant has clearly been greatly affected by the events under consideration by the Tribunal. However, we regarded him as essentially a straightforward and sincere witness and we can accept his accounts of events up to 17 December in its essentials. We are also satisfied, on the basis of the

Applicant's evidence, that there was considerable resentment within the Prison of the Home Office's decision to overturn Mr Mason's recommendation that the Applicant's probationary period should be extended.

"We well understand the Applicant's sense of grievance in those circumstances, but for the reasons which we have given we have reached the conclusion that the conduct of the investigation and the subsequent disciplinary proceedings was not in any way related to the Applicant's race or any matter falling within the Race Relations Act 1976. We must therefore dismiss this application.

"Having seen the Applicant give his evidence, we have no doubt that he has much to offer the Prison Service. It may

well be that, notwithstanding the events with which we have been concerned, he still takes the view that the Prison Service has much to offer him. We hope that the parties can bring themselves to ensure that the Applicant returns to work as quickly as possible."

Wow! If I needed further convincing that deductive logic is the act of putting two and two together to make five, that judgement from the Tribunal provided ample evidence of it. It took a vast amount of patience not to stand up and shout at the top of my lungs, "Logic is an instrument for bolstering a prejudice!" (Elbert Hubbard) at the Chairman; and thereafter hurl Benjamin Jowett (aptly named) like a following uppercut, "Logic is neither a science nor an art, but a dodge" and finally deliver the knockout punch with

Joseph Wood – "Logic is the art of going wrong with confidence." An effective 'Logic' TKO, I'm sure you'll concur.

Certainly, it's easier to appreciate the Tribunal's verdict when considering that anything to the contrary would be disastrous to the Establishment. This becomes more understandable when one considers the oath sworn by senior freemasons to their brethren in the fraternity: "I will aid and assist a companion Royal Arch Mason, when engaged in any difficulty, and espouse his cause, so far as to extricate him from the same, if in my power whether he be right or wrong...."

I was now in a gruelling hide-and-seek game and only too aware of exactly what the late Afro-American Poet Langston

Hughes meant when he lamented in verse: "I swear to the Lord I still can't see, why democracy means everybody but me."

Yet, I was resolved that this hide-and-seek game had to go on; bent on undressing the ogre that was 'race prejudice' of the saintly robes with which it oft deceived the world; committed to exposing its hiding place in the corridors of the Establishment.

There could be no question of my being so naïve as to return to work and expect to be received with open arms, since the reason the policy makers wanted me out of the Prison System was precisely because I was committed to espousing a cause which they wanted to suppress.

~

The decision of the Tribunal reached me on April 10, 1996. A month later, on May 16, in the face of my insistence to take my claims to the High Court; the Civil Service Medical Adviser of HM Prison Service went back to Brownlow Medical Centre for another report on the present state of my health.

The summary of the medical report was that I was deemed to have "a genuine fear of getting assaulted again if he gets back to work in the prison department. I feel that this fear is going to stay with him for a very long time and his chance of returning to the Prison Service in the future is rather bleak."

That was the go-ahead that the Prison Authorities needed to deliver their long-awaited boot, which came in their letter of

August 5, 1996. "I am very sorry that I must write and tell you that on the advice of the Civil Service Medical Adviser, it has been decided that you should be retired on medical grounds," wrote Mr M Joseph of the Conduct and Performance Section.

So that was that. My illustrious career with the Prison Service was officially over. But, I soldiered on in my quest to obtain redress from the High Court, filing my claims against my three assailants and the Home Office in February 1997.

Ironically, it was the same Home Office I was relying on to provide legal aid, since I could not afford an independent lawyer. Lo and behold! I was refused legal aid and forced to pursue my case through one of these 'no win, no fee' lawyers. We reached an agreement of a fee 33.3% of whatever compensation was received.

Following various meetings with my initially enthusiastic lawyer, we formulated and drafted a statement of claim, which in his opinion was superb. After careful consideration, we felt the chances of the case succeeding in an open court, before the glare of the world public, to be very high indeed.

The charges were difficult to refute. They claimed, inter-alia, that the Home Office owed it to the plaintiff (me) to ensure his safety whilst on the premises and to ensure that they did not employ persons who might be likely to assault him; to maintain an internal system of discipline for the purpose of dealing with allegations and/or complaints of misconduct by one employee against another (for which system guidance is contained within the Home Office's own staff handbook) and to give the plaintiff necessary support as an employee; to follow their established procedures as laid down in their own Staff Handbook and to take seriously the plaintiff's complaint that he had been assaulted and battered by the first three defendants.

It was our conclusion that, in breach of their duties to the plaintiff, the Home Office failed to take any steps to ensure his safety during the time of the party and/or, by employing the first three defendants, who were prone to violence.

Further, the Home Office, though purporting to carry out an investigation between the party and the end of 1994, failed adequately or at all to conduct a proper investigation into the plaintiff's allegations.

"As a result the Plaintiff sustained severe personal injury and has suffered loss and damage... In view of the humiliation suffered by the Plaintiff by virtue of the nature, time and place of the said batteries and assaults the Plaintiff claims aggravated damages against the First, Second and Third Defendants and in view of the said failure to carry out a proper investigation, the Plaintiff claims exemplary/aggravated damages against the Fourth Defendants."

This time, aware that it could militate against our case, we were careful to omit any mention of the word 'race' or 'colour' or any imputations to the matter of racial harassment. With this approach, the facts would speak for themselves more eloquently than a direct, bulldozing charge of race prejudice.

For about a year, numerous documents were exchanged between my lawyer and QCs from the Home Office. Then one bright summer morning, I received a call from my lawyer requesting an urgent meeting. We agreed to meet at 13:00 hours at his offices, and when I arrived he took me straight to the nearest pub. Uncharacteristically, he bought me two drinks.

"Listen, Mike," he began. "I like you very much and wish you all the best but I am afraid I am withdrawing from the case."

I stood there feeling stunned, dumbfounded. After travelling this long road, all of the letters back and forth, and the decision of the industrial tribunal, and now we arrive here; we stall at what seems like the last hurdle?

Naturally, my lawyer made the usual noises as to why he couldn't continue with the case - he wasn't as sure anymore as he was originally. But, I wasn't really listening. All I could think about was - *what do I do now?*

Chapter Seven

"Within yourself deliverance must be searched for, because each man makes his own prison"

~ Edwin Arnold

So that was that. My 'sentence' was over. I had served my time and I found myself released back into society; an early release for 'good behaviour' perhaps.

But unfortunately for our society, the prison system hadn't just removed Michael Nsonwu, spitting him back out onto the streets. With amnesia of any of my positive effects that may have improved the inmates within its walls; Pentonville had lost one of its moral compass, thus restoring the distorted equilibrium between the 'screws' and the 'cons'.

I was defeated after trying to provide balance in an unbalanced system. Firsthand, I witnessed the imbalance of the Lumumba situation, and it was a personal loss for me. I took it upon my shoulders to de-escalate a situation between Lumumba and my fellow officers. And I was left with bad memories and second guesses – *Maybe if I'd left him in his cell… maybe.*

***We have** official statistics that puts the Inmate population at 75000-80000 at any one time . What we forget or perhaps refuse to acknowledge* is that people are released and admitted into prisons everyday. If we could do a statistical check over a set period of say 5 years for example, You'll find that the amount of people who have actually passed through the custodial gates is more likely to run into hundreds of thousands. Could we actually make a link between the detoriation of society and the warehouse swingdoor policies of Her Majesty's Prison Service? The mind boggles. The irony is that those convicted and sentenced to custodial sentences are not rehabilitated as was one of my goals, But destabilized and more hateful of society. Thanks in part to the condemning attitudes of the Prison Officers who dispense "justice" and then with no lessons learned throw these angry Individuals back out into the world so they can seek revenge/retribution against any hapless victims that unfortunately crosses path with the recycled and damaged convict.

Continuing the cycle of life, one presumes. And, as ever, the constant 'recycling' of prisoners – just as many entering through the doors of prisons as are re-entering society, worsened by the whole prison experience.

You may be wondering – how is this my problem? What do I care, as long as I bolt my doors at night? Well, what if your child is raped or murdered? Would you care then about the prison system? Otherwise, you think it's the problem of the officers, like Michael Nsonwu, but it's not... It's the problem of family men like Michael Nsonwu. So, it's really all of our problem, and the stark realization of this fact is just the beginning, for making a difference, a change to the downward spiral of society as a whole.

I believe this recycling is making society so much worse. Filling us with fear and dread when faced with our common man. Emotions are crumpled, we don't believe in anything anymore. People are getting more selfish. We're creating this kind of society to live in.

Our youth are disconnected, and life is getting crazier and crazier everyday.The recent proliferation of "knife" culture among the youth emphasizes this. Yet, we can't keep pretending that, as long as it doesn't affect us, it doesn't matter. Rending, rending…
From a spiritual perspective the recognition and acceptance of the Omnipotence, Omnipresence and Omniscience of God makes us realize it's all one, there is no them and us it's all US!

Effectively, we're watching it all slip away, and the solution isn't locking 'em away and throwing away the key. Not if there's a revolving door and they're leaving the prison to re-offend, worse than before.

As a neutral observer, a witness to the goings-on inside UK prisons, more neutral than a officer, more neutral than a prisoner; I was a species all to myself. Sitting on neither side of the fence, but - at times - equally appalled by what I saw occurring in both camps.

Having spent 24 years in Nigeria and 24 years here in the UK I could and would subjectively say that I've struck a balance, best of both worlds et al. I feel extra priviledged to have had this experience because very few people do (Mind you it has not been pleasant rather its been revelatory). Even with the ones that do there's usually an alliance or preference of one over the other. Having had the unique experience of being discriminated against by both sides(The Nigerian side of it is another story) I have come to the same conclusion that the seers and sages of old have always said, that the nature of life itself is dual, the paradox being that without duality life would not exist

Black & White
Man & Woman
Front & Back
Tall & Short
Night & Day

The list is endless and yet we all spring from the same source. Scientist have progressed science into quantum physics and unified string theories they are reaching the realization that there is an underlying energy that is present in everything.

Yes, of course, it was my job and I had to be there everyday. However, I was also doing things that I didn't have to do; talking to the prisoners, sharing spirituality with them, winning their trust, and guiding them down a better path, so when they would be released they wouldn't find themselves yo-yoing right back to the four walls they were presently locked in. At least, it wasn't guaranteed.

Certainly, nobody was paying me to counsel prisoners. In many ways, I was simultaneously exorcising my own demons... I had a stepmother when I was a young boy, and so I understand how people can be derailed. I also wanted to follow in the footsteps of my father – a law enforcement veteran; a good man.

Nevertheless, this made me, arguably, the most neutral observer of all; because I wasn't locked up and I wasn't an officer on a power trip. I knew the differences between becoming a criminal, who has trouble explaining his emotions, and becoming a officer, who stands on the outside, looking in.

But, to fully understand this, one has to grasp the background that I came from. I'm not from the gutters, I was raised as Middle class. I'm considered Landed Gentry in Nigeria, and my family own quite a few buildings and lands. Although, if you're black and you grow up in the UK, it's locked into your brain at an early age that you're different, you're black. So, I wasn't raised to be Second class – the pigeon hole that the British establishment might prefer to place me, along with the other officers I worked with.

Thus, I had a wealth of personal reasons for being in the prison service. As well, I was there as a professional, or trying to be a professional, doing my job and following regulations. Always trying to detach myself emotionally – as hard as it was.

Whereas, a typical prison officer is not very well educated, and comes from a condemning, pious kind of background. Their mindset is: 'I was bullied in school and this is my chance to have a uniform on, and deal with you scumbags... I prejudge you, I condemn you, and I'm going to kick your ass!'

However, my philosophy was that if I believed and I kept within the rules, nothing bad will happen. Moreover, I could make a difference just by being different from the other officers. By being alternative, I would yield different (better) results from the prisoners and for society. And the other officers were beginning to see it happen. In many ways, the officers were losing their grip. A change was in the air.

Though, prison is truly that one last bastion of racism, xenophobia, and closed-mindedness. The establishment, within the establishment, which is like one big family business. Nepotism thy name is HM Prison Service. There are so many relatives working there, it's not surprising that nobody can touch the endemic corruption within the system.

The stereotypes reign supreme. *Once a convict, always a convict*, is the world view. But, all I wanted to do was ask: who is the man behind this convict moniker, what does he believe, what does he do and why does he do it. Because, if you treat them like a con, they become animalistic and self preservation inevitably kicks in, and invariably you yield very different results.

But, for real results, you need consistency. And the prison service needs a serious overhaul. Thus, at the end of the day, this cathartic process changes you, not just the prisoners. For instance, we're constantly bombarded by negativity – prisons are the most negative place on Earth! Every single person who is there does not want to be there. So, the prisoners give you as much grief as they can; it's natural for humans to act out because of their frustrations…

Indeed, this probably explains why officers can be so beastly in return. Becoming animals, too. I saw things in there – unjustlythings, and horrible things. A man charged with raping a two-month-old child… murderers… And this pounds on the conscience and mentalityof the officer; it's a gradual burn. A fuse that is lit and slowlyfizzles away to nothingness.

It's no small wonder that manyofficers dive into forms of recreational escapism – alcohol, drugs. Anything to rise above the hate and monotonyof dealing with societal rejects on a daily basis.

However, we, as officers, have a duty of care for the prisoners in our charge. It's part of our job to keep and rehabilitate this person for the duration of his imprisonment; yet, when I tried to do so, it's possible to upset the apple cart, as I found out the hard way.

The other officers noticed a change in me, as they would watch how I would work with the inmates. Then they would say things, and laugh; sticks and stones. Such as, *Nsonwu floats on the water, and so does shit.*

Yes, you could say, it was a pressure cooker waiting to explode...

Meanwhile, on the outside of the prison, another pressure cooker was building and still is, every day, and still we act like we are powerless to stop it. Like ostriches with our heads in the sand, we hope the problem will go away, but its escalating out of control.

It's a growing problem alongside a growing population of prisoners – set to increase from 81,000 prisoners in England and Wales in 2008, to 96,000 by 2014.

Furthermore, the system is failing - two out of three people who go to prison are convicted of another crime within two years of being released, rising to three out of four young offenders.

Therefore, to cope with overcrowding - which often leads to 'early release' long before their sentences are fulfilled - three U.S. style 'Titan' super jails are being planned, with a £1 billion price-tag, each holding 2,500 prisoners.

Unbelievably, these new prisons are expected to be overcrowded from Day 1, with so-called "planned overcrowding" seeing single cells occupied by two inmates and double cells occupied by three.

Building new prisons – is that really the answer? Or better rehabilitation of the prisoners that we have incarcerated already? After all, they are, essentially, the future prisoners of tomorrow… Like boomerangs, destined to return soon…

Of course, the first step is caring about the state of our prisons, as a reflection of our greater society. Because, in truth, the prisoners are members of society whom we see fit to lock up. But, isn't it so that a pile of dust brushed under a rug is still there. It has not disappeared. To clean up our prisons, we need to start caring and stop ignoring the problems under our noses.

As a result of recycling and heads in the sand, I still run into ex-offenders occasionally. Whereas my former colleagues might fear being stabbed or attacked by the condemned men they 'punished', these ex-cons are usually friendly and offer to buy me a drink. No hard feelings.

Of course, they're not my friends but, from a professional point of view, I understand that they were convicted by the court, by a jury of their peers, sent to prison on this charge, and I upheld my duty to keep and rehabilitate the prisoner.

I did the right thing. Or that was always my intention. But, sometimes, doing the right thing is also about standing up and saying, there's something inherently wrong here, there's a problem, a flaw in this system.

Now, I hope and pray that more people are listening and taking note.

Ultimately, I realized on the very night of my beating a pearl of wisdom that rings true today – the only thing in life that I'm sure of is that I'm going to die… So, why not make this life count?

Since leaving the prison service, this is what I try to do, every day.

Chapter Eight

"The future starts today, not tomorrow."

~ Pope John Paul II

Death and change. The only certainties in a lifetime. Once I had resigned myself to these facts, and the possibility that we are indeed 'all screwed up', I was able to focus on my inner spirituality and "rehabilitate" myself from within.

I recalled the words of Pope John Paul II, when he said: "Anything done for another is done for oneself." I agree with that. And that's why society, as much as the prisoners, needs more rehabilitation to occur within the walls of our prisons – for society's sake.

Yes, society needs the rehabilitating, in my own view. There's little point trying to fix one criminal when the system itself - built on a principle that incarceration is a beneficial form of punishment - is screwed from the beginning. Overhauling the system will be the only way to get any viable results worth writing about.

Though, if we actually make the effort to initiate a groundbreaking change and create a system where you rehabilitate the individual, instead of exacerbating the entire situation by breeding contempt and revisiting the horrors of the victim upon those incarcerated, perhaps we can put an end to this vicious cycle. I truly believe: what we create is what we see. How can they be expected to rehabilitate/renew/forgive/evolve, without spirituality inside their being?

To continue, Pope John Paul II also wisely spoke: "The inalienable dignity of every human being and the rights which flow from that dignity - in the first place the right to life and the defence of life - are at the heart of the church's message... In spite of divisions among Christians, all those justified by faith through baptism are incorporated into Christ... brothers and sisters in the Lord."

Essentially, we should treat a human being like a human being - give him that dignity, no matter what he has done.

Prison gives you an insight into the human mind like no other experience can. People are incarcerated, they're not there by choice; some are broken in the process; some learn to be more cunning. Either way, these incarcerated souls are so disconnected from society, and emotionally bankrupt. Treating them like beasts only serves to alienate them further. To hinder their re-connection into society has, in effect, degenerated society further.

I was pleased to 'connect' with the inmates at Pentonville. Although, I must stress, I don't believe in organized religion – it's the reason for all the problems in the world today - but I do believe in spirituality. Without it, we're nothing more than animals in cells. Because, as long as we're just incarcerating, and not trying to rehabilitate, we will continue on a collision course toward a dystopia of epic proportions.

The future that promises super-prisons and an ever-increasing circle of convicts, enveloping more and more of our population, being recycled and exiting prison - in the majority of cases - worse than when they entered; it's a nightmare. A reality represented in futuristic, dystopic action movies like Escape from New York and Mad Max, where we – the 'innocent' – are the real prisoners and society is the prison; surrounded by violence, people with guns, murders, crime. Unable to leave our homes; paralyzed with the fear of being attacked or robbed…

This 'future shock' may seem far-fetched movie tripe, however it's presently the reality in Nigeria. I feel blessed that the UK doesn't have the capital punishment that exists in Nigeria. Hundreds currently await their fate on death row, where they are finally hung and killed for their crimes… While the Nigerian streets are just as deadly as the prisons, as police shoot to kill, and the robbers shoot back in kind. It's a culture of fear, and you can't even leave your house.

Those Nigerians, who can afford to, live in gated communities. It's like a massive prison! The citizens are putting themselves behind bars! They're scared of the police and scared of the thieves and murderers – but it doesn't matter which is which, as they're all carrying guns and shooting first, asking questions never.

~

Spirituality has illuminated my life, bringing connectivity along with it. We are all interconnected by this spirit and that is what God is. All around us and encompassing, inside everyone. Science tells us that DNA has proven that no two human beings are identical. Still, instead of accepting that, accepting that for there to be life, there has to be differences; we're fighting all these factions of life (being black, green, whatever), cultural misunderstandings, and crimes against one another. And for what? Why can't we open our eyes that those differences produce life; they're inherent.

Your greatest enemy is yourself, and that's the duality of this situation. Yet, we continue to battle the differences – "Unless you're like me, I won't accept you!" How ridiculous it seems, when all of us are unique individuals. It's a paradox and clearly we need to go through a drastic change, an overhaul of our beliefs and societal disciplines, or else face inevitable incarceration (in or out of prison) – trapped inside our own fears and prejudices.

~

Consider that we are all One. You are an aspect of me, dear reader, and I am an aspect of you and everyone else. This connection transcends cultural, religious and race ties. By looking holistically at life and the differences that make it beautiful, surely we see past differences of opinion? Agree to disagree, without saying "I'm going to kill him!"

As I was being held down, pummeled, a head smashing into my face; I thought I was going to die, and I had nothing else to hang onto except God. What am I going to do now? I had a moment of clarity. I could control the million thoughts flowing through my head... watch the thoughts, so to speak... begin to understand controlling them. This helps in handling very emotional situations where anger supersedes.

Anger rears its ugly head and, without clarity or spirituality, it takes over our faculties and wreaks its revenge. And then we must pay the consequences of our actions, even if out of our 'control.' I've seen it time and time again, upon meeting a new inmate, I would say to them, "What happened?" The blank reply would be a typical "Don't know, Guv." A moment of madness, consumed by emotion, he did something criminal, and then he's thrown in cell for the rest of his life (and we end up paying for it).

How does that heal the victim? Unfortunately, in our criminal justice system, we don't do practical things to reconcile these moments of madness... And, ultimately, the incarcerated lose hope, and come out worse off. We might as well shoot them! There is no connectivity between these inmates and society – we're creating a dangerous subculture. A slippery slope to which none of us are immune. If one slides down it, we all slide helplessly as a society.

This is why prisoners need a God or sense of spirituality more than anything and anyone on this Earth. But, also, I can say that everyone needs spirituality, collectively, then we can live and let live, and stop becoming our brother's keeper.

So, let's break the cycle, let's get back to our source, get back to our spirituality. We all come from that, which lies inside all of us. It's our connection with the outside world.

Think about what gives you joy in life? Connection with other people – cultural, traditional groups or the organisations we seek to belong to.

The circumstances of my life, extreme that they may have been, have made it possible to find the spirit inside myself. I've found peace as a yogi, practicing yoga for almost 15 years now. And now authoring this book, I hope that I can have a greater understanding of life, make a definitive impact on the society that we live in, and share my message with the world in the hope of a brighter, safer future for my family and yours.

As, these experiences I've been through

have brought me to these realizations, they've helped to turn something scary and bad, into something positive. For that, I will be eternally grateful. Because, if this has restored hope for one person, then my job here is done.

I may no longer be a prison officer, but I honestly wish that the lifelines that exist between all human beings, the spiritual connection we share, will help to continue to build the much needed rehabilitation in the world today. Reforming people before they need to be reformed – take victims and criminals out of the recycling loop; whether we take them out before they even enter, or during, or after. It has to stop somewhere!

It's a mad world. Accepting that, and accepting that we already have paradise here on this planet, in this life, but we're screwing it up, is the start of solving the problems. We've deviated from what is real. There is more to life than this, and it exists outside of four walls of a cell – whether the cell is real bricks and mortar, or self-created...

Reality check, we live on average 70-100 years, infact the longer you live the more the biological body deteriorates. Within this time span we acquire, determine, experience and live life based on our cultural, religious, traditional understandings and yet we tenaciously cling to material things which we ironically leave behind when we die.

In my humble opinion we never left the garden of Eden, It is still here, look around you Trees still blossom and provide food and oxygen the earth provides for us bountifully from within, most of the staple diets of the world grow freely and were not manufactured what was manufactured was the system of delivery.

Economic systems were created and thus inequalities sprung.

We are born without names and are named by the world via families and ultimately we die leaving the name behind. I find it amusing when people describe the after life from a personalized point of view. I ask the poignant question do you really think you are going to be standing in front of God and saying "You God" me "Michael, Maria, Rashid, Chuck, etc" I think that is the highest form of egoism.. This world we have created is not reality, it is only mind created and until we acknowledge the Spirit, God, Allah, Brahman, Quantum particle etc which underlies all creation, I am afraid we will continue to create the turmoil. Are we going to wake up and realize that all our problems are self Inflicted? Are we going to stop quoting doctrine and realize it is our purpose to act out these doctrines and not the theoretical expositions of it?

Of course, this is just the beginning of the conversation.

What do you think?

www.ingramcontent.com/pod-product-compliance
Lightning Source LLC
Chambersburg PA
CBHW060549030726
47498CB00005B/1320

* 9 7 8 1 9 0 9 3 9 5 1 5 2 *